GRETA

OTHER TITLES BY MANON STEFFAN ROS

The Blue Book of Nebo

GRETA

MANON STEFFAN ROS

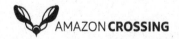

AMAZON **CROSSING**

Published by Amazon Crossing, Seattle

www.apub.com

Amazon, the Amazon logo, and Amazon Crossing are trademarks of Amazon.com,
Inc., or its affiliates.

ISBN-13: 9781662517549 (paperback)
ISBN-13: 9781662517556 (digital)

Cover design by Erin Fitzsimmons
Cover image: © David Lichtneker / Arcangel; © Angela Lumsden, © Kevin Russ /
Stocksy

Printed in the United States of America

For Lleucu Siôn, with heartfelt thanks for hiding under the table

CHAPTER 1

Everything was insane at school, of course. That was to be expected. The school was shut on Monday, and most of our class didn't come in for the rest of the week. I wondered if it made them feel better, or safer, being at home with all that time and their thoughts and the rolling news.

The teachers had already started to panic and were going on about what an important year it was for us and how we had to be strong even though it was all really difficult. Everyone knew that they were talking about exams, but they weren't brave enough to say it because, Jesus, who'd be thinking about exams at a time like this?

In the special assembly we had on the Tuesday morning after it happened, Mr. Lloyd said, "Greta would want us to be strong. We have to carry on. For her." And then a strangled sort of sound escaped from his mouth, and it felt ironic but in bad taste because it sounded a bit like the noise a person might make when they were dying. It was halfway between a cry and a gasp, and then his breath became all swallows and gulps. He stood in front of us, and he wept like a baby, his shoulders quaking as if he was laughing. Fat tears rolled down his face. For a second, I felt the desperate need to laugh, but I held it in until the urge passed, and we all just watched him, bewitched by the spectacle of a man standing in front of us, his heart breaking.

You wouldn't think a bloke like Mr. Lloyd could cry like that. He was a huge, thick slab of a man, nuts about rugby. He wasn't what you'd expect for a head teacher. He swore sometimes and had a hell of a temper. Apparently, the landscape print of the quarry that was up in his office was there to cover a hole he'd punched in the wall after someone had set off the fire alarms four times in a single morning. I wasn't sure I believed that. Especially after seeing him cry like that about Greta.

The difficult moments were the ones you weren't expecting. Stuff like walking from one classroom to another between lessons and passing everyone in the corridors. When Greta was here, she was just one of us—a bit better than the rest, maybe, but no one really took any notice of her because she was there all the time—but afterward, everyone was kind of looking in the spaces where she might have been. And people spoke quietly, half whispering, as if we were already at the funeral.

Everyone cried that week. Maybe the school should have shut all week, because we didn't learn anything at all, except maybe about how grief looks different for different people. I think they only kept us open because school was better than home for some kids. Everyone was in shock, especially in our class. We all stared at Greta's empty chair in whichever classroom we were in, and we all cried. Even the hard kids. A few of the toughest lads had their hoods up and dabbed at their eyes with their oversize sleeves in a way that made them seem even more vulnerable than the ones who were noisily and openly weeping. Crying looks so much worse when you try and stop it from coming.

I was okay.

Honestly, I felt fine. It was a bit like living in a film, as if I'd gone to bed one day and woken up the next morning, and everything was slightly skewed, slightly discolored, like we were all following a script and everyone knew that they had to play a role. And I was no different—cried a bit, but not too much, as was expected of the boys. When Mam had sat me down on the sofa and told me about what had happened to Greta, the palm of her hand on my cheek and her face shining with tears, I played the role of someone who was shocked. I was silent and bowed my head during the minute's silence in the assembly. I tried to look as if I was always holding back tears, pressing my lips together and swallowing a lot. I became who they wanted me to be.

I pretended to feel terrible, but I didn't. Not back then. Shocked, maybe, but my mind and my heart and my guts were completely still. Even when I saw photos of Greta on the telly or the web, even when I thought about her bloody body in the quarry, I didn't feel like crying.

Is that weird?

Or maybe everyone was doing the same—too shocked to really accept it properly, we forced ourselves to cry a bit because that's what people were supposed to do when somebody died. Maybe Mr. Lloyd wept in assembly because he thought that, as Greta's head teacher, it was his obligation. But you don't grieve straight away. You can't.

"Who'd do such a thing?" asked Keira in our English class, running the tips of her fingers along the back of the chair that Greta had been sitting in last week. "I just don't get it." Her mascara ran in crooked black paths down her face.

Nobody had an answer, of course. Nobody knew why someone had killed Greta Pugh and left her body in the quarry, soaked cold with rain and blood.

Most of the newspapers used a school photo of Greta, a picture that was taken about three months earlier. In the picture, Greta smiled kindly, her blonde hair a fold of satin over one shoulder. She wasn't wearing much makeup, and the only jewelry she had on was a small pair of stud earrings—diamonds, I think, tiny and sparkling, the sort of earrings a little girl gets when she's just had her ears pierced. She looked sweet and kind and sort of childlike. People seemed to find it especially terrible that someone had killed such a pretty, innocent-looking girl.

I couldn't look at that picture without remembering the tiny details of the day it was taken. For some reason, my memory had stored the details like scenes in a film, but no one else talked about it after Greta died, no one mentioned how odd it had been. The girls all sitting in class, balancing compact mirrors or phone cameras on the desk in front of them, showing their own reflections. The thick, cloying scent of nail polish, and Keira and Ela swapping their school-approved stud earrings for longer, dangly ones and then pushing a few bracelets onto their wrists, looping necklaces around their necks to rest against the pale skin of their collarbones: crucifixes and love hearts and hard, shining initials.

But that's not what Greta did.

She took a wet wipe from a packet and removed all her mascara and eyeliner and lipstick. She swapped the huge gold rings in her ears for those tiny glittering studs with pink gems in the shape of love hearts. She closed the top few buttons of her shirt, although they were usually always left open, showing a hot-pink or animal-print bra. She pulled her hair from the high ponytail and shook it loose before combing it with her fingers, her short pink nails clean and neat.

The other girls were trying to look older, sexier. But not Greta. She was attempting to look younger, more innocent.

"Look at *you*," said Keira, and Greta stared at her own reflection on her phone screen. "You look about twelve!" And Greta grinned, proud of herself. She had achieved her aim.

That's what Greta was like. It's just that in the aftershock of her death, no one seemed to remember that. As soon as she'd taken her last breath, we'd started slightly misremembering her, as people always seem to when someone dies.

◆ ◆ ◆

Mam was waiting for me when I came home from school the first day we went back after it happened, still in her pajamas since the night before, an empty mug on the floor beside her. She was watching a news channel on telly, and I turned to the screen to see the same school I'd left fifteen minutes earlier. A woman in a black suit was standing by the bus stop, clutching a microphone, her face straight and serious.

". . . Greta Pugh was a model student, popular, and kind . . ."

"You okay?" asked Mam, and she put her arm around me. I pulled away. We weren't that kind of family. Mam and I didn't kiss or hug, and I didn't want to start now.

"Yeah. Why are you in your pajamas? Didn't you go to work?"

"They canceled. I was meant to be with Eleri Jenkins this morning. She's in the same group of friends as Liz, Greta's mam, isn't she. Poor thing. She said she couldn't cope having anyone over, not with what's happened to Greta." It irritated me, the way she spoke about the people that she worked for as if they were friends. She was a cleaner. They didn't care about her. It was just that she charged less than anyone else, and did a good job, and never spread gossip when someone had filthy habits or an unhappy home. She was paid a pittance to make their already perfect lives easier, and that was not friendship. "I don't know what I'll do on Thursday when I'm meant to be cleaning Liz's. She's not gonna want me about the place."

The telly showed live footage from outside the school. You could see the graffiti of a dick that someone had drawn on the twenty-miles-per-hour sign in the car park.

"Was school awful, Shaney? The story's been on telly all day. There was a class photo—you were in it."

"Which one?"

"Last year's."

Shit. I'd bleached my hair a whitish blond last year. I looked awful in that photo, pale and pathetic and too long for my body, and now it was being seen by everybody in the world. Typical. And what a rubbish claim to fame.

"Is there anything to eat?"

Mam turned to look at me properly then. It wasn't a nice feeling—Mam barely looked at me at all usually. People don't when they live together. But now she stared for a while, as if she couldn't quite remember who I was, as though I wasn't quite making sense.

"You sure you're okay?"

"Of course I am."

That night, Mam put a couple of frozen pizzas in the oven, and we binged on the grotesque misery of news channels. All they showed was news about Greta. It was a weird feeling, especially when they showed places that we knew. Sometimes, Mam would call out, "Hey, look, it's Ogwen Bank!" or "That's Parc Meurig!" And then the people on the news would talk about this awful thing that had happened, and Mam went back to crying. She was a messy crier, all snot and swollen eyes, and it made it difficult to sympathize with her.

The photo of Greta smiled innocently at me through the screen. I felt suddenly guilty for thinking mean things about my mam. I should make an effort to think kinder thoughts.

I watched in silence. It was all so odd. This was happening here, now.

It's a funny thing, watching your home, suddenly exposed, listening to strangers trying to describe your village. Of course most of the people watching would have never heard of Bethesda, so the reporters had to sum up a whole community in a few words. A few of them said things like "Here is a gateway to the beautiful tourist hot spot of the Snowdonia mountain ranges," but most weren't so kind. Stuff like "This is a sleepy village whose main industry, slate quarrying, has long past seen its heyday" or "Unemployment has reached a record high in northwest Wales, and Bethesda, near Bangor, is suffering the effects."

"Who the hell do they think they are?" Mam asked when she heard that. And even though it was all true, what they were saying, even though I knew how my village must look to outsiders, I knew what Mam meant. The only things the reporters could see were a few boarded-up shops on the main street, or the rubbish that rose in brightly colored drifts in the car park on Cae Star. They didn't see all the warm, friendly, brilliant things about Bethesda. They didn't want to see. They thought the fact that our town wasn't full of BMWs and Range Rovers went a long way toward explaining why someone here had brutally murdered a sixteen-year-old girl.

They were desperate to believe that something like that could never happen to them.

"Bastards," I said, and for once, Mam didn't tell me off for swearing.

◆　◆　◆

Later on, I got a message from Dion.

Don't say a word. Remember.

I didn't reply.

CHAPTER 2

"Bloody hell," Gwyn said as we walked to school the next day. He flipped up the hood on his coat as if that was enough to make him invisible. "The cops are like dog shit around here. Everywhere."

It was true. Round every corner, on every street, there were police watching everyone coming and going, as if they expected the murderer to strike again outside Brenda's Café or outside the school gates. It was broad daylight.

It got worse as we neared the school. There were cops by the gates, cops by the bus stops, cops in a ring around the photographers and reporters that were huddled like a mob on the pavement opposite. In the days after Greta's death, cameras followed each and every one of us as we walked into school.

"It's a bit bloody late for all this," Gwyn added, huddling down deep into his padded Adidas coat as if he could hide from the cameras. And he was right. I couldn't remember the last time I'd seen a police officer out on the streets before all this happened. They all looked a bit shell shocked, as if they'd been drafted in from another country and had no idea where anything was or who lived here. Usually, they only came out if there was fighting or if one of the parties in the park got particularly loud.

"It's like they're suddenly on our side," I agreed, passing through the throng of people. Whenever we'd seen police officers before, they'd have snarling faces, hands twitching by their sides, trying to resist the constant urge to reach for their Tasers. They'd hated us until last weekend, and now they were meant to protect us from the hungry snapping of the cameras.

It was like being famous. The reporters were everywhere, hiding their faces behind gun-black long-lens cameras. Everyone started dressing tidier, wearing more makeup, walking a bit slower into the school in the hope that they'd be noticed.

Of course there were cops at school too. But they were mostly not in uniform, the men in square suits and the women in somber colors—black, gray, brown. It was obvious which one was the boss. It was the woman who had spoken to us at the very beginning, in a short assembly at the end of that first day back, and she'd told us that it was *extremely* important that we shared *any* information we had about Greta.

"Even if you don't think it's relevant," said Detective Chief Inspector Karen Davies. "We need to know everything about Greta in order to understand what happened to her."

To be honest, I didn't get that. What could any of us say that would make anyone understand the fact that she'd had her brains bashed in? If they found out that she was the school bully, would that explain her death? What if she was a drug dealer? And what if she was just normal—not the angelic, intelligent, beautiful girl we all saw on the front pages of the newspapers, but average?

DCI Davies was a small woman. At the assembly, she'd pleaded with us all to "Please, call me Karen," with a sympathetic head tilt and a sad smile. But she looked like the type of person whose own parents called her Ms. Davies. Everything about her was neat—her suit, her short dark hair, even the small solid steps she took when she walked through the school corridors. I wondered who she'd be at home, how a person who was that stiff could ever relax. I couldn't imagine going up to her to talk about Greta. *Did you know that . . . ?* or *I don't know if you know this, but . . .* She had that whole TV-detective vibe nailed. It felt like a low-budget, bad crime drama was being filmed in our school, and Greta was the tragic and absent star of it all.

◆ ◆ ◆

There's something you should know about people like me.

We're invisible.

You probably wouldn't understand. I imagine that you're one of the others, one of the people that count. You live in a nice, big house, a house your mother and father bought. Your home isn't the property of someone else, rented out to you for a sum you can't really afford. You have your own room, and there's no mold on the walls. Maybe your parents are in a relationship with one another, but if not, they're with *someone*. They have someone to love, or they choose to flit between lovers, and that's their choice because they know that they will always, no matter what, be desirable to someone. They work. You go on holiday sometimes.

You excel at one thing at the very least. You might struggle with math or fitness, but there's one thing, maybe more, that you're very good at. You have a talent, which means you have some hope. You have barbecues in summer, and you're ensconced in the type of family that has new pajamas on Christmas Eve so that your mother can post a photo on Facebook. Your mates might fancy your mam—as she's pretty because she has the money to be.

Gwyn and Ela are those types of people. Greta was like that too.

We're not.

Not Dion and me. Not Keira, really.

You don't really see people like us; we exist simply to make up the numbers in your classes or football teams. We're very like you in some ways: we speak to you, and go out with you, and sometimes we all convince ourselves that we're similar, that everyone on earth is created equal. But if we disappeared, no one would notice, nor would they really care. *Shane who?* they'd say, and then, *Omygod, yes, SHANE! I forgot about him! I haven't seen him for ages!* After a few months, they would have forgotten my face completely.

Depressing? Yes, sometimes. But it isn't all bad. Because as I said, we're invisible.

We tend to be together most of the time, Dion and I, and we're nothing but a couple of lads in joggers and hoodies. We stand at the bottom of your road, sit in the corner of the park, walk between the little Tesco and the fish-and-chip shop and the park.

Maybe I've got it wrong—maybe it isn't quite invisibility. You see us, don't you? But you don't realize. We're not significant enough for your brains to take note of our presence.

So . . .

When you pass us in the car, you don't notice that we see you and your direction of travel and the exact time at which you're traveling.

When your mam buys one bottle of wine in Spar, another in Tesco, and another in the corner shop, we notice.

When your dad's parked in a lay-by for a long time after he's told you that he's working late again, we're the ones skulking around, smoking, and it's us that hear him saying to whoever's at the other end of the phone that she's sexy and gorgeous and that he can't wait to put his mouth on her body.

As I said. People don't think. If DCI Davies was a better detective, she would have come looking for people like me. People who know far more than they ought to.

It was raining at break time, but we were still meant to go outside. It was only spitting rain, the kind that would have been fine to play football in it. But the last lesson before break was English, and when the bell rang, Miss Einion said, "You can stay here for break time if you don't want to go out." Miss Einion isn't usually that kind of teacher—she always gives the vibe that she doesn't like people, especially young people.

Most of our classmates went out anyway—one or two needed a smoke, and a few were meeting their mates from other classes. Mary, one of the girls who always tended to be on her own, looked like she was going to stay, but when she saw that it was only our group that stayed, she glanced at us with her huge Disney-animal eyes and gathered up her bag to leave. Poor Mary. She wasn't a friend of Greta's, but she'd seemed to shrink into herself even more since it happened, shoulders stooped as if she was trying to fold into her own body.

"Miss Einion'll have a breakdown before half term. Guaranteed," said Ela, nodding at the door after Miss Einion went off to the staff room to get herself a coffee.

"Calm down," replied Gwyn.

"She was nearly crying all lesson! Didn't you notice?"

"Everyone's nearly crying in all the lessons. She's no different. It's just the shock."

Dion reached into his bag for an enormous packet of crisps, and he opened it before plonking it in the center of the table. We didn't usually share, but everyone was trying to find tiny, unfussy ways of being kind to one another. I helped myself. Sweet chili flavor. My favorite.

"Where is she now?" asked Ela suddenly. I hated the way she ate her crisps. She'd lick all the taste off them, all the salt and tiny flecks of chili powder; then she'd put the crisp on her tongue, and she'd suck it. All the other boys fancied her because she was curvy and had straight jet-black hair and looked a bit like someone you'd see in a music video. I wasn't so sure about her. She was plastered in makeup, which always made me think of how all that gunk would rub off on my face if I ever kissed her. I wasn't sure what she actually looked like. And anyway, I suspected that a girl like her would never go anywhere near someone like me. There's no point wasting time fancying people that you'll never be good enough for. She was a bit of a snob.

"Who?" asked Gwyn.

"Who do you think? Greta!"

Everyone went quiet. I think Ela knew straight away that she'd put her foot in it, because she looked around at everyone in a bit of a panic.

"I mean, is she in the hospital? Or with the funeral director? Or the cops? I don't know!"

"She's probably in one of those massive cold drawers you see on *CSI*," Dion replied quietly, his eyes wide. "In a bag with a zipper."

You could almost hear the whir of people's minds as they imagined that. I could see it on all our faces, and I looked down at the floor, the same as I did when I was in assembly and I was pretending to pray. They were all thinking of Greta, like I was, motionless and cold in a dark drawer in the hospital in Bangor. Perhaps her skin had turned blue, like the dead bodies on telly. Maybe her face was all caved in. Her head open and bloody. Red congealing darkly in her blonde hair, shining and sticky.

When I looked up, Dion was staring at me. His face was empty, as if he felt nothing at all. It was terrifying.

Keira moved her hand over to the chair beside her. Greta's chair. She wasn't crying, but I could tell by the look on her face that it was because she was *too* sad. She probably had it the worst of all. I hadn't known before then that there was a sorrow that was bad enough to stop you from crying, but I saw it then, and recognized it.

I tried to remember the last time I cried, I mean really cried properly, not just to prove that I had feelings. But it was far, far too long ago.

That night, when I was meant to be asleep, I looked online on my phone to see what people were saying about Greta.

My room was small and cramped, but I quite liked it that way. It was more like a nest than a bedroom. I never ever had friends over. We always hung out outside, or in bus stop shelters if it was raining, so I didn't ever have to worry what people thought about my room. I had lots of fluffy blankets on the bed and four pillows even though it was only a single bed. My clothes were crammed into a chest of drawers that I covered with another fluffy blanket, and my TV and console were on a shelf at the foot of my bed so that I could lie in bed and play or watch. The walls were painted a pale cream that had become dirty looking over the years, but most of it was covered in posters of anonymous city skylines or supercars that I'd never ever see in real life.

I used to have posters of footballers on my walls, but I had nightmares. All those faces watching me as I slept. I was only little then.

Instead of lying under a duvet like other people did, I'd make a sort of burrow in my blankets and then settle underneath my softest one, which had a picture of a wolf howling at the moon on it. That would be how I slept, and usually I slept soundly, half listening to the hum of cars on the main road a few streets away. But not since Greta died. I'd curl up and shut my eyes, try to listen to the sound of the village around me, but somehow, I'd always start wondering about Greta. About how cold she must be, how uncomfortable, all stretched out in a body bag or a coffin. And I knew it was stupid—of course I did, she couldn't be cold or uncomfortable; she was dead—but it still made me feel odd and a bit cruel, being curled up and warm and alive in my bed.

So I looked at my phone and hoped it would make me sleepy.

It was exactly the type of thing you'd expect—most people were kind, and a few said that she was too young to be out so late on her own, that Bethesda was a rough place, and that this kind of thing happened here all the time. Of course no one could remember the last time a murder had happened here. It wasn't within living memory. But still, people wanted to believe that it was a violent, unhappy place.

I lay in bed, the screen of my phone lighting up my face. I could hear Mam watching TV in her bed. She'd finally switched over from the news channels and had gone back to watching *The Real Housewives*. Sometimes she fell asleep with it on—she said she liked having voices around as she fell asleep.

I looked at the website for one of the most popular newspapers and read the story about Greta even though I'd read it twice before. There were hundreds of comments left by people from all over the world.

15

Sleep tight beautiful angel xxxx—Margaret, Milton
Keynes.

And this is why the UK needs guns. Her killer
needs to be found and taken out.—Kevin M, Kansas
City

RIP to Greta, and sympathy to her devastated family. So sad to see such a beautiful young woman
taken too early.—Michelle, Perth, Australia.

I read each and every one of the comments. All of them. It was half
past one by the time I laid down my phone to charge on the bedside
table and shut my eyes. Even then, I didn't sleep straight away. I couldn't
stop thinking about the weird way those strangers online were talking
about Greta.

The darkness in my room was suffocating around the bright, harsh
light of my phone screen.

Almost every one of them had referred to the way she looked.

*Beautiful. Angelic. Blonde. Blue eyed. Stunning. Pretty. A stunning
young woman. An innocent beauty.* Somewhere in my head, this all meant
something—the fact that everyone seemed to think that this tragedy
was more poignant, the loss of this life more wasteful, because Greta
had been beautiful, because her eyes had been blue and her hair blonde.

There was some sharp, ugly truth about that, but I was too tired to
see it. It was too soon to think too much—just keeping my head down,
living from day to day, that was enough.

CHAPTER 3

On Thursday, something unexpected happened.

It was nothing, really—or perhaps it was something, maybe one of those things you don't realize its significance until you've moved farther away and you're looking back.

I arrived home from school, but Mam was out. That wasn't unusual—she worked long hours, sometimes until eight in the evening if it was summertime and people wanted their holiday homes cleaned. She hadn't left me a note, so I helped myself to a peanut butter–and–banana sandwich and lay back on the sofa.

I sat there for a bit, enjoying the silence. I hadn't known it before Greta died, but there isn't a whole lot of silence in the immediate aftermath of a great tragedy. It takes time for people to be okay with being quiet again. It's as if they think noise will occupy their minds enough, take a bit of the sting from whatever's happened. Yes, people talk in quieter tones, barely more than whispers sometimes, but it's constant.

At home, Mam always had the TV on, whether she was watching it or not. At school, we spent all our lessons either being droned at about wars or chemistry or desperately sad books, or we were talking when we were meant to be working.

This was the first time I'd heard total silence since the night Greta died.

It was nearly a week since Greta died, and school was a completely different kind of place now. Everyone tired so easily. Of course there was lots of crying, and a lot of cops, and the photographers were still at the school gate. But it's strange how quickly unusual things become normal. Within a few days, we couldn't quite remember what life had been like before, when there weren't cops prowling the perimeter fence by the Astroturf and when we had classes where no one cried. We didn't even raise an eyebrow anymore when someone started weeping and left the room. It was what we expected.

And Greta, too, seemed somehow changed in our minds—she became sacred, every memory of her a treasure. Her year-eight math book was unearthed from somewhere and was passed around the class under desks, like some kind of forbidden holy book, even though it was full of incorrect answers and Greta had hated math. A picture of a dandelion she'd painted last year that had been hanging outside the art class since then had become a place of pilgrimage—girls were always huddling around beside it, speaking in whispers, sometimes crying.

But the biggest change was the teachers. Mr. Lloyd must have told them to be kind to everyone, especially our class, so no one ever yelled or told us off. After four days, none of us bothered doing any home-work. Half the girls said they were too depressed to do PE, and though Mrs. Doyle was usually a cruel woman who got a kick out of humiliat-ing her pupils, she simply nodded sympathetically and said nothing. In the English lesson, Guto Wyn described Roger from *Lord of the Flies* as a bit of a prick, and instead of going mental and giving him detention, Miss Einion just sighed and said, "Okay, that's enough." In a way, it was great—but in another way, I wished everything was a bit more normal so that we all knew where we stood.

I had almost fallen asleep on the sofa with my phone in my hand when Mam came in. She was in her work clothes, and she looked exhausted, her whole face sort of heavy seeming. She traipsed in and stared at me for a few seconds before going into the kitchen to put the shopping bags down.

"All right?"

"Yeah. You?"

"Don't ask." I heard the click of the kettle being switched on and the soft thud of the kitchen cupboards opening and shutting as she put away the shopping she'd bought with the wages she'd just received. "Bloody hell, Shane, can't you tidy up after yourself? There're crumbs everywhere!"

"Sorry."

I heard her sigh then, just as the kettle boiled and clicked itself off. I was the one who was uncomfortable with the silence—I almost reached for the remote to switch the TV on just so that someone would say something.

"Sorry, Shaney," she said, as I knew she would because Mam was good at apologizing. "I'm in a horrible mood today."

It wasn't like her to be so tetchy—we were all right, Mam and me; we never really argued. She must have had a very bad day.

I didn't find out until later what had put her in such an uneasy temper. Not until she brought me my dinner and we both sat in front of the telly with bowls of tomato pasta on our laps, the steam like ghosts in front of our faces as we watched the news. Greta was on the screen again, of course, and there was a clip showing her parents, all hushed voices and sparkling tears, sitting in front of a poster of *that* picture of their dearly departed daughter, begging anyone with any information to please, please come forward and tell the police. Cameras flashed at them—they looked as if they were trapped in a lightning storm. The silence between their sentences was awkward, as if they had forgotten their words.

I noticed that Mam had stopped eating.

"You okay?" I asked.

"They make me sick."

The words seemed to escape from her throat like a choke, as if they were something she had to get out so that she could breathe again.

I put down my fork. It was so unlike my mother to say such a thing—and especially to say it about those parents that had just lost their daughter so violently. She'd been cleaning for Greta's family for years. She liked them and had always spoken kindly about them. Mam was one of the good ones, one of the nice ones—always kind, usually smiling, never had a bad word to say about anyone, even the ones who deserved all the most pointed, sharp, bladed words.

"Mam!"

She started crying—just one sob that sounded like something finally bursting inside her. I stared at her. I probably should have gone over and put my arm around her, but I didn't.

"Mam?"

And she told me what had happened.

Mam always went to the Pughs' house on Thursday mornings. She'd leave our house by about nine o'clock because she'd wait to see me off to school, and then she'd have a coffee, watch the news, and do the breakfast dishes before she headed to work. Then she'd drive up to Bryn Mawr. By then, Greta would be at school and her parents would be out. Mam would clean and tidy the house and do the laundry and any ironing that needed to be done. Mrs. Pugh—Liz, she was called—would leave her money in an envelope under the antique clock on the mantelpiece, the one that ticked the time away heavily, sounding tired.

Bryn Mawr was a big old farmhouse with a lot of land—almost an entire mountain, looking down at Bethesda as if it knew better. The Pugh family was rich enough to employ people to do most of the dirty work. Although Kelvin, Greta's father, was a farmer, and although he woke up at dawn every day and went out on his quad bike to survey his mountain, he was always back by midmorning. They employed farmhands to fix the fences, muck out the sheds, and do all the other dull, dirty jobs that would have made him a real farmer. Mam said that he'd come in just as she was cleaning the kitchen or one of the bathrooms. He was always polite to her, or so she said—a nice, simple kind of man. Almost nice enough to appear stupid.

Liz Pugh was one of those rich, polished women who always smiled because they never had any reason not to. She was tall and beautiful, her blonde hair always falling as if she'd just stepped out of a salon. She worked in a posh clothes shop—they call them boutiques, actually, although that just means posh clothes shop—in Bangor, but I think she did that because she was bored, not because she needed the money. She was one of those people who pretended to be hard up while going on several foreign holidays a year and paying 150 pounds a pop to some salon in Chester to chop a few inches off her hair.

People adored Liz Pugh.

I could see why. The way she always smiled and gently teased everyone, the way she always seemed kind, as if everyone in Bethesda was her best friend. Even at a parents' evening or a school concert, she managed to chat with everyone, make everyone giggle. Together, she and her husband looked like the perfect couple. They linked arms when they stood together, and it always looked so natural, so heartfelt. Many, many people counted Liz as their best friend. She had a way of leaning in when she talked to people, then making eye contact and smiling softly. She made people trust her.

You've already guessed that I don't like her. I didn't swallow this perfect-woman, perfect-wife, perfect-mother act of hers, and that was partly because of what happened at the last parents' evening.

At our school, parents' evening always happened in the school hall, and the teachers all sat by their desks around the edges, their backs to the walls, with the pupils and their parents waiting their turns to have an awkward, five-minute, coded conversation about how well we weren't doing. *Eloise can be a little introverted* meant that Eloise had no friends and ate her packed lunch alone in the restroom. *Frankie is certainly spirited* meant that Frankie was a hyperactive psychopath. Not that any of them would be saying anything like this about Greta, of course. She and Liz were there, but not Kelvin.

Liz was chatting to one of her friends, someone's mother, a woman who dressed like Liz and sounded like Liz, but her hair could never fall quite so perfectly; she could never quite get the understated fashions right, and she knew that she would always fall short. It was enough for her just to be associated with Liz—she didn't have to feel that they were equal. They were both expensively dressed in creams and beiges and white, as if they were about to go for a meal, not standing in the tired, slightly smelly school hall. I wondered if parents' evening counted as a social outing for parents.

Mam and I needed to see Mr. Francis, the geography teacher, so Mam led the way, passing Liz in the throng.

"Saaaaaaam!" said Liz, flinging her arms around Mam before kissing her lightly on the cheek. "So lovely to see you!"

"Hi," said Mam. She isn't the kind of woman who hugs anyone. Her cheeks began to flush—the reaction of an eleven-year-old girl suddenly given attention by one of the popular girls—but Liz didn't notice. She turned to introduce Mam to the other woman.

"This is Sam, and she's *amazing*," Liz told the other woman. "One of my favorite people in Bethesda! You two would get on like. A. House. On. Fire!"

Mam smiled, and her whole face brightened. I don't know if she'd ever heard herself being described as amazing before, especially not by someone with such social clout. Then Liz turned her gaze to me. "And Shane! You've grown! I'm sure they're saying *brilliant* things about you here, aren't they; you work so hard!"

Then I noticed that Greta was standing behind her, scrolling through her phone. She was waiting for her mother to stop chatting shit so that they could go and speak to some teachers. A part of me unexpectedly pitied her—I hadn't realized before then that Greta wasn't caught up in the whirlwind of her own mother.

I smiled politely, but I didn't reply. Liz knew nothing about how I was doing at school or about how hard I was working. I could be staying at home every day smoking and playing *Call of Duty* for all she knew. This was all nonsense. But there was something in the way Liz was smiling that looked as if she really cared, as if she really meant it.

That was the gift she had. It was impossible not to be taken in by her, just a bit—impossible not to like her.

She was a lot like her daughter in that way.

Mam chatted with Liz and her friend for a bit before making her excuses when she saw that Mr. Francis was free. But she didn't look as though she really *wanted* to leave, just as though she felt like she ought to. Liz said goodbye to my mother with a kiss. "We'll *have* to get together for a coffee soon!" And then Mam and I moved away. I thought that Mam would never be invited for that coffee, not really.

And that's when, through the voices and bustle and the squeaks of shoes on the floor tiles, I heard Liz turn to her friend and say in a low, breathy voice, "Poor thing. She's my cleaner."

Bitch.

I felt my insides becoming cold and hard. That woman, that smiley, gentle, friendly, rich woman had dared to pity my mother for being her employee. *Poor thing?* Mam didn't need her pity. I turned to look back, but Liz had leaned into her friend, and they continued their conversation in hushed tones. But it was Greta that caught my attention. She was gazing up at her mother with absolute contempt. She had heard the comment about Mam, too, and knew how awful her mother sounded. And then her eyes fell on mine, and we stared, just for a second, no smiles exchanged, no frowns. But for a second, I understood Greta perfectly, and we both knew it.

On the Thursday following Greta's death, Mam decided not to go up to Bryn Mawr to clean as she'd usually do. She had sent Liz a text a day after Greta died—something like *Thinking of you all xx.* She hadn't expected a reply, and she hadn't received one. Mam had been anxious about what to do—I'd half listened to her as she loaded the washing machine at home, or as she sorted out the recycling, speaking her thoughts out loud—"I can't just go up there to clean as usual, can I, as if nothing has happened? They probably don't want to see anyone at all, never mind the cleaner . . ." She decided to wait for Liz to get in touch before she ventured up to the old farmhouse again. Mam never ever wanted to be in anyone's way.

But that Thursday morning, at half past nine, Mam's phone rang. She was enjoying a rare morning off, watching rubbish on the telly as she ate her toast. Someone from Manchester had had a horrible make-over on one of the lifestyle programs—Mam was thinking how her dress looked like it would crease after washing. She didn't rush to answer the phone—it was usually some charity or scammers trying to blackmail her into giving money she didn't have.

Her heart skipped a beat when she saw the name on the screen. It was Liz Pugh.

"Hello?"

"Sam, when are you coming? This house is in a state."

Mam couldn't believe it. Liz's voice was clear as a bell, as if nothing had happened.

"Liz . . . you're . . ." Mam failed to finish the sentence, and the silence filled the seconds, all the unsaid words.

"Are you there?" Liz asked after a while.

"I'm so sorry about Greta," said Mam finally.

A long, deep, slow sigh. "Thank you."

"I didn't think you'd want me . . ."

"Can you come over? Now?"

"Yeah, course."

Mam was at Bryn Mawr within ten minutes, anxious and jittery. Would they all be crying? Were there going to be cops everywhere, and if there were, was Mam supposed to ignore them or say hello? Was she meant to clean all the rooms, even if there were people milling about?

There were a few cars parked in the farmyard, so she knew there must be visitors, and Mam didn't know if this was better or worse than having only the family home. All the cars were newer and grander than my mother's battered old Fiat, but she sat there for a minute or two, feeling safe inside the old car that had carried her along so many miles.

As she always did, Mam went in through the back door. The house was quiet, and the utility room at the back—where the cleaning stuff was kept, and the washing machine and vacuum cleaner and all the coats and shoes—was empty.

Mam took a deep breath and ventured into the kitchen.

Liz barely looked up at her. Greta's mother sat at the dining table, which was covered with the pictures and prints of several newspapers, a gruesome tablecloth dotted with Greta's grinning face and bold, ugly headlines: *Dead Welsh Schoolgirl Was "Model Student"*; *Searching for a Monster—Who Killed Greta Pugh*; *A Welsh Angel: A Community Mourns*. No one else was in the kitchen, but there were days of chaos smeared and crumbed on the countertops—dirty dishes, smears dried into hard chips on white porcelain; the remains of old meals, bread curling at the edges and sauces starting to stink; crumbs on the floor.

"Thanks for coming," said Liz, her voice surprisingly stable and firm and her eyes still focused on the screaming headlines about her poor murdered daughter.

She looked so normal.

Better than normal, Mam thought. Her hair was done perfectly, and she was wearing makeup. She was one of those women who had a signature scent, some expensive perfume bought for her in big chunky bottles on birthdays and anniversaries, and Mam could smell her, along with the rotting food and the faint aroma of that morning's breakfast toast and coffee.

"Liz . . . ," said Mam, taking a step toward her. "I'm so, so sorry. I don't know what to say."

Liz looked up as if hearing this was a great surprise to her. She nodded slowly. "Thanks," she said, as if she was thanking Mam for washing a silk shirt or polishing the dresser. "Could you do the whole house, please? People are starting to come here to share their condolences.

And Bedwyr has come home from university. You know what a pig he can be."

"No problem," Mam whispered, thinking that Liz must be in terrible shock to be acting this normally. There was a certain edge of danger to the situation, as if Liz could start wailing or smashing things up any moment. Grief was unpredictable, and *this* kind of grief—well, Mam didn't know it well enough to hazard a guess at what it might be like.

"And if you could take some laundry home with you to iron," Liz added. "There are piles in the laundry basket. You'll never get through them in a day."

And so Mam did her work. She moved around the house as quietly as she could and tried not to get in anyone's way. People came and went, but very few of them took any notice of Mam—only one or two people nodded an acknowledgment in her direction as they were ushered into the parlor. Bedwyr was in the living room watching Netflix, but he didn't even look up at her, never mind saying hello. (He couldn't blame his grief, either. He'd always been a snob.) Mam didn't see Kelvin at all, but she heard him through his study door—the only room that she never cleaned. He was speaking on the phone, his words muffled and his voice teetering at the edge of tears.

After cleaning and tidying, there was only one place left to go.

Mam stared at the door.

There was a small wooden sign on it, a memento of early girlhood, with a simple line drawing burned into the wood, of a horse and a name in swirly, looping letters. *GRETA.*

Her bedroom.

Mam had no idea what to do. She knew the room well—it was painted gray, with glitter in the paint, and everything in there was soft and luxurious, every single item carefully chosen. Unlike Bedwyr, Greta was a naturally neat person, and apart from vacuuming and dusting, changing the bedsheets, and occasionally taking away the odd empty glass or coffee mug, Mam had never had to do much in there. But even opening the door felt like an imposition now. And Mam told herself, there was no way that Liz would want her daughter's room cleaned . . . not after . . .

"The bedsheets need changing." Liz appeared from the parlor, carrying a laden tray of empty teacups. She was tending to yet more visitors, who needed another round of tea and coffee. "And I think her school uniform needs washing too."

"Don't they—the police—don't they need . . . ," started Mam, her voice inflected like an apology. She had no idea how to speak to Liz.

"The police have already been here. They said it's fine for us to clean."

Mam nodded, feeling that the last thing in the world she wanted to do was to cross the threshold into that room.

But of course she had to. That was her job.

So Mam went into the bedroom of Greta Pugh, who hadn't yet been dead a week, and she cleaned and polished every inch of the place. Tears tore down her face as she vacuumed the carpet, which had a few biscuit crumbs that Greta had accidentally dropped while sneaking forbidden snacks between meals. She wept as she changed the bedsheets, which smelled a bit like Greta's shampoo and the peach perfume she wore. She dried her eyes with her sleeve as she wiped a few freckled spots of makeup off the sink in the en suite, pulled out the hairs from the drain hole in the shower, and cleaned off the spots of toothpaste from the mirror.

She felt as if she were removing the last few remnants of Greta from the place that knew her best.

Then Mam sat on Greta's bed, not yet feeling quite ready to face Liz to say her goodbyes. She didn't want anyone to know she'd been crying—after all, no one else seemed to be upset, and it might look strange that the only tears spilled for Greta Pugh were the ones wept by the cleaner.

Mam looked around and saw Greta's schoolbooks, the same ones as I had at home—*Blood Brothers* and *Macbeth* and *Lord of the Flies*. She looked at the framed photos on the wall of Greta and her friends, at the straighteners still plugged into the wall, at the shiny, high-heeled pair of red shoes by the wardrobe, white stickers still clinging to the soles, waiting to be worn.

Mam listened to the silence of someone who had gone. She thought that there was nothing in the world as sad as a dead young woman's bedroom. And something inside my mother became hard as she heard Liz moving through the house, speaking softly as she walked her guests out. My mother was in no way hard—if anything, she was gentle enough for it to be a weakness, gentle enough to make her vulnerable. But she found an edge within her that day, sitting on a dead girl's bed, because Liz's grief didn't seem enough.

◆ ◆ ◆

"People grieve in different ways," I said to Mam after she'd told me what her day at Bryn Mawr had been like. "Liz is probably still in shock." I surprised myself, standing up for Liz like that, because the truth was I didn't really believe what I was saying. I knew more about her than Mam ever would, and none of it good. But I didn't like to see my mother being cynical. She always thought the best of everyone—I needed her to stay that way.

"You're probably right," said Mam unhappily before piping up again. "Except, no. Something's off with her, Shaney."

"You don't think *she*—?"

"God, no! Of course not. I wouldn't ever think that! And maybe *I'm* in shock and not thinking straight. God knows what she's going through . . ."

"But?"

"I don't trust her. I don't . . . I don't think she's *good*."

◆ ◆ ◆

Mam's instinct was something she should have trusted. She hadn't always listened to it in the past when she should have done.

She didn't know how much I knew about Greta's family.

No one knew how well I knew Greta.

They didn't know it was that moment at the parents' evening that brought us together. For Greta, my catching a glimpse of who the real Liz was felt like enough of a basis for a friendship. Someone, even a nondescript blank face like mine in a classroom, was suddenly treasured because I knew what she was really like.

I wished people would have known. I wished they knew to say *I'm sorry for what happened to your friend* or *I know you two were close; I hope you're okay.* But nobody knew anything, because in the twisted, manipulated world she lived in, Greta wouldn't have been allowed to have a friend like me. Unspectacular. Poor. Male. It meant no one would ever know.

And now she was gone, and the only person in the world who knew we were anything to one another was me.

It was important that things stayed that way.

CHAPTER 4

"Don't get changed, lads," said Mr. Lloyd. "There won't be a lesson today."

"Eh? Why?" asked Gwyn, who was always full of nervous energy and lived for break time football and PE lessons. This morning's stagnant math and history lessons had left him aching for movement.

"DCI Davies wants to see you in the hall," replied Mr. Lloyd. I could see the pinpricks of sweat pushing their way through the pores on his forehead. There were damp patches under the armpits of his shirt. He was moving, always—one of these people who was never still, always shifting weight from one foot to the other, or scratching a point on his neck, or cracking his knuckles. He looked as if he could do with a rough game of rugby to calm his agitation. "Sorry. C'mon, follow me." He left the changing room, his shoes click-clacking on the dirty tiled floor.

Most of the boys were annoyed, but I hate rugby. Shame, really, because I was named after a rugby player called Shane Williams after Mam and Dad met on some drunken, rainy night out after Wales had won a big game. But I prefer football, and anyway, Dad hasn't been allowed to see me for years. Not that he'd want to anyway.

Everyone went to the hall, where the girls were already waiting, most of them delighted not to be forced into playing field hockey. Mr. Lloyd and DCI Davies stood in front, and there were two coppers in uniform sitting at the back. Miss Anwen was there, too, her face now permanently etched into an anxious frown. I don't know exactly what her job was, but she was always at school, talking to the sad kids and the bad kids and the completely bloody mad kids. What a job. I wonder if she'd ever thought, when she sent in her résumé and filled out the application for the job, that she'd have to deal with the fallout of a murder on top of a whole generation of kids messed up by selfish and broken parents. Her job must have felt like being a firefighter with only a thimbleful of water.

"Come on, lads," said Mr. Lloyd. "Sit down. Karen wants to talk to you all specifically, what with you being in Greta's class."

We found seats at the front of the hall. Usually, the year sevens sat here, and it was weird being back in the little kids' seats. I suddenly felt big and long, folded up in a plastic chair that used to be too big for me.

Dion sat beside me.

I sat up straighter and tried not to look at him.

"A few things, guys," said Karen, smiling kindly at everyone. "Firstly, I just want to make sure that you're all okay?"

A few weeks earlier in English class, Miss Einion had taught us all what a rhetorical question was. "It's a question that doesn't expect an answer," she had said, with that annoyed, disappointed kind of tone that her voice always carried when talking to us.

Greta had put her hand up. "I don't get it." A comment like that from anyone else would have sounded rude, but there was something about Greta's open, kind face, her questioning eyes, that always seemed genuine, as if she really, really wanted to know the answer.

"Well . . . something like How many times do I have to tell you?" explained Miss Einion. "That's rhetorical because, although it's a question, it doesn't need an answer. Or something like Who cares? You could reply to that one, I guess, but the question doesn't require a reply."

Greta nodded as if that explained it, and Miss Einion moved on to talk about something else. But my eyes stayed on Greta, on the slight crease in her forehead, not *really* understanding, her own question not *really* sufficiently answered. I suppose she thought that all questions could be answered, really, even the ones that didn't seem to require a reply.

I wasn't sure if "I just want to make sure that you're all okay?" was a rhetorical question from DCI Davies or just a stupid one. What answer was she hoping for? Everyone remained silent. The sound of someone laughing far away drifted in through the open window.

"I'm sure it's hard. Really hard. Remember, please—Miss Anwen is here for you, and there's counseling available all day, every day to anyone who needs it. The counselor is in the deputy head's office, and you can just pop by there when you feel the need. Just for a chat."

I knew that a few girls had already visited the counselor, but I'd have preferred a twenty-four-hour game of rugby in the pouring rain to anything like that.

It was obvious by now that DCI Davies was, in fact, hoping for some kind of reaction from us, because as she stared at our faces, each one blank and silent, she seemed a little uncomfortable. "And we're here, too, of course. If anyone can think of anything that might be of interest to us. You might think it's nothing . . . but it could really make a difference. So. Please. Tell us."

I saw a few of my classmates exchanging looks when she said that, a few words whispered under their breaths. I didn't know what they were saying, but I was guessing that it was something to do with Greta and the way it was difficult to tell what was important information and what wasn't. *She had a can of Diet Coke every single day. She had a habit of playing with her hair, putting it in a ponytail and then letting it loose and then putting it up in a ponytail again and then plaiting it when she was trying to concentrate on something. She chewed the side of her mouth when she was trying not to laugh.* There is so, so much to say about a person, all of it, and none of it, relevant.

"Look," sighed DCI Davies, her voice more normal now, dropping half an octave, as if she was just one of us, chatting to her mates, and not a copper looking for information. "We're starting to get a fuller picture of Greta now. The Greta you knew. You know what I'm on about—the real person."

A thick silence fell heavily. I felt Dion looking at me, and I raised my eyes and looked back at him.

How much did they know?

"No one is perfect. And we need you to be completely honest. We've got a far better chance of finding whoever did this the more we get to know about her. And that includes the things she might not have wanted her parents knowing about."

Thoughts started hemorrhaging through my head. There were so many memories, so much to say—the exact things that DCI Davies was desperate to know about, and the exact things that I would never ever tell a copper. And I'm sure each and every one of us had private, hidden, secret things that we would never divulge to this boxy, neat police officer. The very thought that anyone would tell her anything seemed ridiculous.

"I'll be around all day today," DCI Davies added. "Come and see me for a chat, eh? The smallest detail about Greta could be a clue that really cracks this case open."

A wry smile threatened to curl my mouth, but I resisted it. She was trying to talk like a cop in a TV drama because she thought that we'd be impressed by that. But there was something in her voice that told us that she knew she wasn't getting anywhere. We weren't going to talk.

Some things, you just don't say.

We weren't meant to leave the school grounds during break time or lunchtime, but of course we did. Not every day, but it always happened on Fridays, and our gang always went down to Brenda's Café on the main street. We'd been doing it since year nine—it was one of those things we did a few times, thinking we were grown up and cool just because we were old enough to buy lunch in a café. It became a tradition. A ritual.

Now we all walked down the side path and off the school grounds via the back street, knowing that was the only way we wouldn't have to pass the massive throng of reporters and photographers who were still stalking the front gate. We were just chatting—Gwyn was going on about the Premier League and how Arsenal were looking like an amateur club at the moment, and a few of the others were moaning about the Welsh homework that none of us had done yet. Brenda's Café was half-empty—the only customers, as always, old people, bent over the Formica tables and sipping their weak tea, nibbling their tea cakes. It was the same crowd every day. In Brenda's, people swapped news with people they'd known since school—who had married, who was having an affair with whom, who had died, and who had given birth. I loved Brenda's. It was more like someone's living room than a café. Most people went to Crust up the street; that was nicer but more expensive.

That day, everyone looked over at us as we sat, even though we came here every week and were used to being just an invisible part of the café crowd. Everyone was silent for a bit, and I saw one of the old men who was there every day, look down at his hands, his face creasing deeper with sadness.

"Ah. That poor girl," said Brenda, looking at the empty chair that Greta used to sit in. Of course. To them, Greta was the girl who came here with us every Friday, ordered a ham-salad sandwich and a can of Dr Pepper. Always sat in the same chair, always angelic, never forgot to say please and thank you. Because of our Friday ritual in this cheap café, every one of these regulars was connected to Greta—*She'd come into Brenda's every week, you know, chat with her mates and that. We never really talked, but she knew us. Lovely girl. Kind.*

After Brenda took our orders, Gwyn nodded in the direction of the empty chair.

"Did you notice that she always did that?" he asked.

"We all sit in the same chairs in here," Ela replied flatly. "We always have done."

"Yeah, but wherever we went, she always sat facing the door. D'you remember? She was always looking out."

He was right. At school or in cafés or in Maccies in Bangor or in the Cricket Club at a party or even if it was just on a bench in the street on a Saturday night, Greta always sat where she had the best view. Facing the world, not her friends, eyes flitting outward, as if she was expecting someone. Why had I never noticed that until Gwyn said it?

"So what?" asked Keira. "She liked watching people."

"I'm not saying it means anything . . . ," Gwyn started.

"Well shut up, then," Dion snapped impatiently. "You're looking for clues in every single bloody thing, just because she's dead. Give it a rest."

Brenda brought us our lunches, and everyone fell quiet. No one thought too much about what Dion had said, because that's what he was like—like a little terrier, silent until he snapped.

Keira was halfway through her tuna sandwich when she said, "Maybe we should talk to that DCI Karen."

"And tell her what?" I asked.

"What Greta was really like. You know, what *we're* really like. They have no idea, really, do they."

Everyone looked up at her, everyone except for Ela, who looked down at her plate and shook her head. "I've told you, that's not what Greta would have wanted . . ."

"That's not what she would have wanted when she was alive!" replied Keira, trying to keep quiet enough so as not to attract the attention of the old folks in the café, who had gone back to chatting tiredly to one another. "But maybe we should tell the truth now. Just so that they know . . ."

"No." My voice was flat. "We can't. And you know as well as I do what Greta would have wanted. This way, she gets to be remembered as an angel, a perfect woman. Almost *too* perfect. Not normal."

Suddenly, a memory flashed into my mind. It felt different from the rest, because it had burst into my head and, for a few seconds, had jostled for space, taken over, as if there was no room in my thoughts for anything else. I'm sure we'd all had the same thing, all of us who knew Greta, these vivid, colorful, powerful memories. But this memory was mine, and no one knew that I had it.

The quarry, and the sun trying to pierce its way through the dense, heavy clouds. The slates still slick with that morning's rain, but the dark, wet patches slowly drying out at the edges. Greta in a bright orange raincoat, her hood covering her head even though it had stopped raining. I could see that her hair was wavy and straggly under her coat—she hadn't bothered to straighten it.

She was smiling at me, and crying too.

"Shaney! Did you bring me gummy bears?"

"That's what she was like," Ela said back in the café, and I smothered the memory. "She's gone, Keira. We can't change that. Let her be, now."

When someone dies, for a while, the memory of them brings so much more hurt than it does joy.

"But somebody's killed her!" said Keira in a small choking voice, and though I hated myself for it, the only thing I could think of was how irritating Keira was, with her fear and tears and the fact that she went on and on about things she could never change. She had loved Greta so much, and that made her seem pathetic.

Greta wouldn't have been so weak.

◆ ◆ ◆

I'd been avoiding Dion for days, but that night, I agreed to meet him in the park. That's where we'd go in the evening if it wasn't raining, because it was in the middle of the village but was private enough to feel like it was far away from everywhere. We had to walk past the old bakery, long boarded up and covered in bad graffiti—*Lowri loves Rhods* and *CYMRU!* and *The system hates you*—and cross a footbridge over the river Ogwen, and there was a playground with swings and a slide and a seesaw, but there were also miles and miles of footpaths through the woods. You could walk to Tregarth along one path, or Mynydd Llandygai, or even over the mountain to Rhiwlas if you had a lot of patience and about four hours. Along a different path, you'd walk and walk until you reached the lane, and that led to the quarry.

We'd always meet by the swings because that's where people went when they had nowhere to go. But there were other people there that evening, some year-nine girls and year-ten boys, so Dion and I walked down to the river. He'd stolen a few smokes from his mother's packet, so even though we didn't really smoke that much, we both had a cigarette. The night was completely black, like the screen at the end of a film, and only the tiny orange cigarette tips and the tiny white waves of the river could be seen.

"D'you think Keira'll talk to that copper?" asked Dion.

"No. She'd only make herself look bad. No one's gonna talk."

"You've been quiet." I couldn't see Dion, but his voice was flat, as if he'd had enough of my nonsense.

"Mam doesn't want me going out. You know what they're like. She thinks I'm at Gwyn's house now."

"Everyone thinks there's a murderer out there."

"Well, there is, Dion."

That was strange because, as I said it, I hadn't really thought about it before. Everyone was going on and on about the dangers and saying that we weren't to go anywhere alone, not the park or the quarry or the river, unless there was a big crowd of us. I'd thought of it as just one of those stupid things adults say because they like to feel in control of their uncontrollable kids. Another tactic they used to get us to fear the world. Because of course there was no danger to us, was there? Greta was dead, yes, but she wasn't like the rest of us. She was . . .

She was *dead*. And somebody had killed her.

"You told anyone about Saturday night?"

"Don't be soft."

"Make sure you don't. There's no point, Shane, d'you understand?"

"I'm not thick, am I."

"No, but you're too nice. She's gone. Nothing we say can change that."

"What if it happens to someone else?"

Dion sighed. I saw the tip of his smoke becoming brighter as he took a drag. "There is no one else. There was only Greta."

CHAPTER 5

I couldn't get the quarry out of my head.

I dreamed of it—disjointed dreams without a story to them, just the feel of the slate, the jagged edges of the mountain. The quarry had been looking down at my home throughout my life, just a part of the landscape, like the sky and the mountains, the main street and the pylons. All of a sudden, I was aware of it, up there on the mountain like a blinded eye.

When I'd started secondary school, our first history lesson taught us about the quarry—how it had been the biggest slate quarry on earth once, how there had been a big strike there over a hundred years ago, too long ago to feel relevant, and how Bethesda had stood up to the big bosses and tried to balance the wealth.

I wished they would have succeeded.

The strike wasn't what preoccupied my thoughts, though—it was the quarry itself. It was the way a mountain had been there once, grassy and wooded, its face smoothed out by nature and icebergs and weather a long, long time ago. And that men had stuck explosives inside that mountain and had blown it up, time after time after time, misshaping it a little bit more every time. They'd hacked away at the slate inside it, that smooth, pretty, bruise-colored stone, and had broken it down to make slabs for roofs and gravestones for marking the dead. Men had spent entire hard, tough, dangerous lives breaking down the guts of that place, and now it remained a hole instead of a hill, a gouged-out marker of a mountain that was long dead. They had disemboweled an entire mountain.

After Greta's death, I suddenly felt the weight of that long-gone mountain, as if our whole community had spent its entire history in mourning for what used to stand there. To walk along a slate path was to tread on a dead thing. That quarry, looking out at the village always, was judging what we had done. And Greta, now, had joined it in death—she was the broken mountain; the purple bruises of the slates were hers.

In the first week after Greta's death, I became obsessed with working out what the police knew about that Saturday night. I had to know how much of the information they had. The different threads of what I knew tangled up in my mind come nighttime, when I couldn't sleep. The papers were full of the story, and the news on TV. Some parts were obvious, and some parts, I couldn't work out how the police could possibly know about them. Not that it really mattered. They still didn't know the half of it.

I don't like writing at school, probably because I'm not very good at it. But I *do* like writing. Making lists, that kind of thing. It was something a teacher told me years ago, when I was in primary school and was finding it hard to say what I meant, and everyone was going on about how important it was that I talk to someone after what happened with my dad. The teacher said that I should write things down, just for me. It helped, sometimes, to get my brain in order, when my head filled up with ugly, dark shapes that couldn't quite fit into my mind.

I hadn't made a list for a while; I think I'd sort of forgotten that it was something I did, something that helped. But I found myself drawn back to it then, fetching a pen I'd borrowed from someone at school and never given back and an untouched notebook that Mam had inexplicably bought for me as a Christmas present.

I decided to make a list of what the cops knew about Greta on her last Saturday night.

- In the morning, she'd gone shopping to Llandudno with her mother. She was bought some new clothes, and they went for lunch (I say lunch, but both Greta and her mother were strict with themselves when it came to food, so it would have been a green salad or maybe just coffees. Greta loved food, she once told me, but she only allowed herself to eat sweets or chocolate or bread when things were particularly bad, and she always felt horrific afterward, as if the food was literally weighing her down.)
- After they returned home, Greta went to her room, saying she had homework to do. Her social media accounts show that she posted a selfie at 15.27—Greta smiling, sitting cross-legged on her bed. She wore a black hoodie, hood up. (People think that hoods are cool on people who have money, and intimidating on people who do not. Greta looked cool; In my hoodie, I looked threatening.) That selfie racked up hundreds of likes and a string of comments—*You look so hot! Gorgeous xx Nice top! C U 2nite x.*
- Through the afternoon, Greta sent messages to the group chat she had with Ela and Keira. The police had copies of these messages, and although I hadn't seen them, Ela and Keira had told everyone of their contents—gossip about going to the park that night, what they were going to wear, Ela moaning about her parents and Greta replying sympathetically. The messages were completely average. There was nothing to indicate that anything was wrong.
- She had dinner with her family at half past six—homemade kebabs and salad, and because her family were modern and liked to think they were progressive, wine too. (Another one of those class markers—drinking with your parents is fine when

it's expensive wine sipped in the dining room of your detached, expensive home, but it's irresponsible when it's cheap alcopops in social housing.) Liz and Kelvin Pugh later claimed that over their meal, they had discussed the summer holidays, and the possibility of going to Paris. Greta had been enthusiastic. She said that she had a lot of homework to do that night, and so would not be going with them for a long walk as Kelvin had suggested.

- At half past seven, Kelvin took Greta to Bethesda in the car, where he dropped her off outside Ela's house. Ela and Greta walked down to fetch Keira, before they all walked down to the park.

- Greta was wearing jeans, white trainers, a pink T-shirt, a white sweater with the word ADIDAS on the chest, and a brand-new denim jacket. She was carrying a small red cross-body bag, which contained a small bottle of vodka, her phone, makeup, and a bank phone charger in case her battery ran out.

- There was a big crowd down at the park, but Greta stayed with our gang for most of the evening. The police, I think, have correctly deduced that the members of our gang are Greta, Keira, Ela, Dion, Gwyn, and me. They seem to think that the girls are the closest-knit group, and that us boys occasionally join them. We were sitting on a small rocky outcrop among the trees, but there were many people around us, mostly from our year at school. There were people coming and joining us and making conversation all the time.

- Everyone was drinking. Everyone was chatting too, and everyone was drunk, at least a little bit, and a few were stoned. I think there was a fight between two year-nine girls at one point, but it was nothing to do with us—we barely even registered it. There's always a fight when people are drinking.

- The plan was for Greta to spend that night at Keira's house. That happened a lot, because it was too far for Greta to walk home.

- No one can quite remember what happened at the end of the night. It happens like that often—people wander off, people fall asleep in the trees or disappear for a while with someone. Gwyn had copped off with Ela in the early evening—that happened a lot too, I don't know why they didn't just get on with it and become boyfriend and girlfriend properly. Keira had snogged an older girl from the sixth form class, who had her own car parked behind The Bull, and had disappeared there with her around half an hour earlier, but no one was worried. People always disappeared when they copped off with someone. Dion and I were chatting with girls from our year, but we weren't having much luck with them.

- A few people in the park said that they could remember seeing Greta at the end of the night. She was chatting with everyone, laughing, and was very, very drunk. As in, slurring her words and falling over a bit as she walked. But most of us were the same. She didn't stand out. She seemed happy.

- One girl, someone from year eight, was walking out of the park in the direction of the main street just before eleven (she knows the exact time because she was meeting her mother for a lift home). She says she saw Greta walking unsteadily along the path that led through the trees and to the quarry. The girl remembers Greta having her bag with her—she was struggling to close the zipper.

- After finishing whatever she had been doing, Keira went looking for Greta, but she wasn't answering her phone. The police had searched Keira's phone records, and saw that she had tried nine times to call Greta that night. But the girls have something they call *the girl code*. If one of them goes AWOL, it probably means they've pulled and that they'll be staying somewhere they shouldn't be. When that happens, friends lie to parents about the whereabouts of their children. So Keira went home, thinking that Greta was misbehaving and having a great time with some bloke. This wasn't usual for Greta, but that meant nothing—everyone starts somewhere, sometime.

- The next morning, Keira tried to phone Greta again, but it went straight to voicemail, and the messages sent to her on social media were left unread. Keira wasn't worried to begin with—Greta had probably passed out drunk in someone's house, her phone out of battery.

- Liz tried to contact Greta around midmorning to arrange picking her up and bringing her home. After receiving no reply to her messages, she phoned Keira, who lied, still determined to stick to the girl code and not get Greta into trouble. She said that Greta was in the shower, and that she had overslept. Liz said she'd be there to pick her up at two, before a late Sunday roast. That's when Keira started to panic. Greta had to be back by two, or everyone would know that they had lied. She sent a message to our group chat, hoping, I think, that Greta had spent the night with me or Dion or Gwyn. That was, of course, highly improbable.

- Around the same time as Keira was messaging us, a man from Tregarth had gone for a Sunday morning run. He had turned up the lane by Ogwen Bank, up toward the quarry, and he slowed to a stop at the top of the hill to catch his breath. That's where the lake comes into view, and so he walked over the slate to have a look down. Then he turned back and saw something a little farther up the mountain, something that was more than just dead slabs of slate. Something, or someone. He jogged over, thinking that someone might need his help, but of course it was too late. Greta had been dead for hours.

- Her bag, and everything that was in it, was missing. Her clothes were intact—no one had attacked her sexually, and there were no signs of a struggle. She had a single, massive wound to the head where she had been hit once with a large, heavy object. There were hard, heavy slabs of slate all around her, each one a possible and potential weapon.

- The police were called, of course, and as they jumped in their squad cars and raced to Bethesda, Keira was phoning everyone, trying to find Greta.

- Kelvin, Greta's father, turned up to pick up his daughter, and Keira reluctantly had to admit the truth—she wasn't sure where exactly Greta was, but she was sure that she'd be okay. She was probably fast asleep in someone's house, and about to wake up with a horrible hangover. But as Keira was making these excuses for her best friend, the sound of police sirens came screaming across the Sunday morning silence as they headed for the quarry. Later on, Keira said that Kelvin had looked in the direction of the noise, and that his face "became all folded up, like a paper bag." He turned to Keira and asked, "She'll be okay, won't she?"

- One of the few truthful things Keira told the police was that it would be that moment, above all others, that would stay with her—those words, and the edge of desperation in Kelvin's expression as the nightmare was just beginning to threaten them all. That, Keira says, is when she began to think that something truly awful had happened.

That's it. That was my list of what the police knew. I took all evening to write it out, and I kept it under the mattress in case Mam found it and thought it was weird. But I looked at it every night, and tried to think what the police were thinking. To them, it looked like Greta had copped off with someone or had arranged to meet someone, that she was drunk and had stupidly lost her friends. They probably thought that some stranger had taken her, had killed her after she'd rejected them. Something like that.

I really hoped that was what they were thinking.

Because they had no idea.

It was absurd, the things they didn't know.

How could they *not* know about Kelvin, her controlling father, who was sometimes laid back and let her go out and wander about with her friends and sometimes would monitor her phone and messages and Google history? How could they *not* know that he'd be so extreme, sometimes forbidding her from wearing tight or revealing clothing and sometimes buying those exact outfits for her?

How could they not know about the grasping way Liz would clasp a wineglass in the evening, every evening, drinking until her mind was dulled? How did they not know that there were stories about her that sounded like they came from a cheap novel that people would just read for kicks, or a movie that no one would own up to watching?

They knew about the A grades on Greta's school reports, the way she liked her bedroom tidy; they'd seen the clothes she liked wearing, and they'd gone through her music playlists to see if there were any clues there. They'd searched her computer and read her creative-writing assignments in case she'd slipped up and given them some new information. I couldn't help but smile sadly when I thought about it. It was funny and tragic, the way they thought they'd find out the truth about her in the things she had left behind.

That was the thing about that DCI Karen—it didn't matter how good she was at her job because she would never meet Greta. She would never get to know what she had really been like. She only had the clues that Greta had left for her, and nothing else. The police were clever; it's just that Greta was even cleverer. She'd been so smart, so *tidy* with the information she'd left for the police. As if . . .

As if she'd planned it all.

◆ ◆ ◆

"What song are you having at your funeral?"

It was a religious education lesson, teaching us about the ways different religions deal with death. The student teacher who was taking the lesson was one of those young, cool guys who wanted to be everyone's best friend. He wore Nirvana and Red Hot Chili Peppers T-shirts to school with a casual shirt draped over it. We let him believe that, yes, he was cool—that made the lessons easier. He was, of course, a pathetic, desperate people pleaser, but he was nice enough. He wasn't significant enough for any of us to remember his name.

"'Going Underground,'" someone said, as if that was original. No one laughed.

"I want the Welsh anthem," said Gwyn. "I love listening to it before rugby games." I couldn't say it at the time because the thought was weird, but I thought it would suit him. Everyone would cry. He'd probably have the Welsh flag draped over his casket like some kind of war hero.

Keira wanted a ska tune that her mother had played to her a lot when she was a baby; Ela wanted something by Taylor Swift because it would make everyone cry. Neither Dion nor I answered the question, but I secretly thought it would be up to my mam what song was played, because she'd be the one that was most upset and she'd be the one listening to it. If that meant it was a crap song from the nineties, then so be it.

I never considered the fact that Mam would probably die before me.

Ela nudged Greta—"What would you have?"—and Greta wrinkled her nose and shook her head as if the whole idea wasn't to her taste. "Don't be stupid!" she said. "When I die, I'll be old, and all the music I like now will be old fashioned."

"Good point!" said the student teacher, pleased that we were having a conversation about something that was very loosely based on the lesson we were meant to be having. He'd probably considered it a great success.

"How could I choose now?" Greta said, her fingers wrapped around a purple sparkly pencil, like vines choking a tree. "I haven't even lived my life yet!"

CHAPTER 6

I hate funerals.

Like Auntie Cath's funeral back when I was in year seven, when the vicar stood in the crematorium in Bangor, droning on about her in that hushed chapel voice as if he was talking about Mother Teresa. "A kind, giving woman, always smiling even through her woes . . ." And I had looked around me, wondering if we'd come to the wrong funeral. I remembered the last time I'd seen Auntie Cath, when she turned up to our house, off her face on something, her eyes rolling so that the whites were wide and bulging. She'd screamed in fear that there were men with knives for fingernails hiding under her bed. That was a few hours before she climbed into that same bed she was so frightened of, her skinny body full of too many tablets, and a few days before someone found her curled up in the fetal position under the duvet, her hand still clutching a bread knife. She had died terrified of the monsters lying in wait under her bed.

So I knew that funerals were rarely anything like the people they were meant to commemorate. They were just a ritual, punctuated by prayers that no one knew whom they were for.

I didn't want to go to Greta's funeral. I knew that it would be heaving, horribly impersonal, and that there would be reporters and cameras to capture grief as if it were just a story. And anyway, who wants to go and watch other people cry? It's not respectful.

"Don't be so bloody stupid," said Mam. "We have to go."

"Why? Nobody's going to notice if we're not there." I pulled on my school shirt. It was a Thursday, but the school was shut for the rest of the week so that everyone could go to the funeral and take some time to grieve. I didn't have another smart shirt I could wear. Mam had bought me a black tie in a charity shop, and I had my black school trousers and shoes.

"That's not the point. Come on, now."

Mam was wearing exactly what she had worn five years earlier to Auntie Cath's funeral and the same as she had worn to the rare nights out she'd had in the meantime. Black trousers. Black shirt. High heels—those were unusual for her—and a black jacket. But some of the blackness had faded from Mam's jacket in the wash, and from my trousers, too, so they were more like a very dark gray, the color of a storm.

We looked terrible.

The funeral was at Jerusalem Chapel on the main street, which was a grand old building, huge and hulking, built when people believed. It looked different, felt different, swamped by hordes of people in black, everyone keeping their voices low as if sound itself was disrespectful. Beyond the chapel gates, photographers and television cameras recorded every move, tracked every single symptom of grief. They wanted to get shots of pretty, young women crying, and they succeeded. They wanted to see people broken, made faithless by this tragedy, and they got what they wanted, of course. They didn't know the history of the chapel or what it was really like. That's where we had our school carol concerts. That's where Greta had gone to Sunday school when she was young, to learn all about God and Jesus Christ and sin. Generations of nonbelieving teenage chapelgoers had scratched their initials into the backs of the pews, having complete faith that there was no God watching them.

Of course there were just too many people. Mam and I had arrived early, but we only just managed to find a place to sit, up in the gallery and at the side. The whole gang was there, dotted around the chapel—Keira with her mother; Ela and Gwyn together, their parents on either side of them; Dion with a few lads from the football team. I think almost everyone from school turned up. Mr. Lloyd was sitting almost at the front. His suit looked as if it was strangling him.

At the back of the gallery, I spotted Call Me Karen sitting somberly in a suit that looked like all the other suits that she wore every day. There was a man in a long black coat by her side, and I wondered for a bit if he was her husband—but no, it made more sense that it was a plainclothes police officer. They tried to look like the other mourners, their faces suitably straight and gray. But I watched Karen for long enough to see that she was watching everyone. Her eyes darted around the chapel, watching all the faces, peering over the gallery at Greta's family, all her friends. She would have been wondering if Greta's murderer was part of the congregation. If they were hidden in plain sight, trying to act as people are meant to act at the funeral of a murdered girl.

I wondered if she felt strange, attending the funeral of someone she never knew. If she felt like she was intruding. I wondered if people like her ever took any time off their horrible jobs, flitting from tragedy to tragedy, just to feel the sadness.

Karen suddenly turned her face to mine and caught me staring. I held her gaze for a while before turning away and hoped, with a fizz of anxiety in my belly, that she wouldn't read anything into the fact that I was watching her.

The organ began to drone, and everyone turned. The coffin was rolled in—one of those modern woven ones like a basket, a bright, summery yellow. It was covered in flowers, pretty flowers, not the type you buy in garages or the garish ones people give one another on Valentine's Day. These looked like the flowers that grew in the fields around Gerlan or under the trees in the park or in the shadow of the stone walls on Greta's father's land.

I'm not the type of bloke who cries, but those flowers did something to me. I swallowed hard, tried to hold the tears back, wrong-footed by my own feelings. The flowers looked perfect for Greta.

"Aren't they pretty," she told me once, wrapping her fingers around the bright-yellow flower of a dandelion, cupping it around the stem.

"Dad hates them. But look at that yellow! They're just so perfect." She had a lit cigarette between her lips, and the ash at the end of it was falling lightly as she spoke.

"You can eat them," I said. "You can eat the flowers and the leaves and the roots and everything."

And she looked up at me and laughed before taking a drag of her cigarette and holding it between her fingers. "Don't be weird, Shaney."

I forced myself to quash the memory. Not here. Not now.

If she had been allowed to choose her own funeral flowers, I'm almost certain that she would have picked the exact ones that were now on her coffin. I wondered who had chosen them. It surprised me that anyone in her family had such good taste or that they knew her that well. This one thing, this one, final choice they had made for Greta—it had been the right one.

The flowers were the only things that felt right in the funeral. Mr. Lloyd's eulogy—well, he didn't know Greta any better than any head teacher knows their pupils. The Bible reading didn't even sound like a language that we understood, never mind being a comfort or hope in this mess. There were a few hymns, of course, ones we only knew because we sang them at assembly at school. The older people sang like they meant it; we all just mumbled.

I watched Greta's family in the front few pews.

Liz was a beautiful woman—a few of the boys from our class had teased Greta about that, and she was always ready with a barbed reply, "Of course she's sexy; she's my mother!" Liz was leaning into her husband, sniffing her tears throughout the service. He, on the other hand, was completely still and silent. He didn't cry at all, not as far as I could see, and he didn't reach to hold Liz's hand or to comfort his son. Bedwyr had always been a prick, but I felt for him now—his mother leaned on his father, and Bedwyr stood a little apart as the hymns were sung, by their side but also somehow alone. It must have felt strange to suddenly be an only child. There was more family—a grandmother and two grandfathers, uncles and aunts and cousins that weren't anywhere near as pretty as Greta had been. Bedwyr looked around at everyone, at the crowded chapel, seemingly faintly surprised at all the people who had come to say goodbye to his sister. He didn't look as if he'd cried a single tear.

The second hymn was a Welsh one—"Calon Lân," which means clean heart. Everyone chooses that hymn at weddings and funerals because anyone who speaks Welsh knows it. They play it during rugby matches, and people sing it when they're walking home from the pub, the alcohol giving them permission to insist upon being heard. I don't like it. It starts with *Nid wy'n gofyn bywyd moethus*—I'm not asking for a life of luxury—and then goes on to say that all you need to sing is a clean heart. Not asking for luxury. How could you not? A clean heart is good for sod all when you're hungry and cold.

I sang, of course. Mam was crying by then. Most people were. Only a few of us held back.

But instead of thinking about a clean heart, I was remembering a party up in the quarry, when everyone had felt brilliant because it was school holidays and it was hot and we were all either drunk or high. The older boys had brought their cars and parked in a circle, headlights on, and everyone was dancing in the middle, lit up like the moment before a car crash. The sun had just set over the purple slates of the quarry, and the sky was as pink as kissed lips.

Greta was dancing.

I don't know why I'd paid any attention to her at all—I was going out with a girl from Bangor then, Eva, who was sixteen and too kind and too wild and too experienced for her age. There were loads of girls there that night, all twirling in the car headlights, but I remember Greta best of all. She was drunk or had taken some uppers, because she was dancing with her entire body as if there was something inside her that had to be shaken out. She and Keira had put glitter on their faces, and Greta's cheeks were shining as if she was crying sparkly, beautiful tears. She was grinning as she danced, and oh! she was pretty. Perfect. But there was a dangerous frailty about her, too, as if that smile was about to crack like a heart. Most people just saw a beautiful girl, but some of us recognized something else in her, something that made us concerned for her.

Only family were allowed to go with Greta to the crematorium after the service in the chapel, but there was a funeral tea at Bryn Mawr later in the day. It was clever of them to arrange it like that, really, because if they'd had the tea in the village hall or in Crust, everyone would have gone. It was a trek up to Bryn Mawr. Only the determined mourners would bother, or the ones who really wanted to see grief close up.

"Come with me to help," said Mam as we waited in line to leave the chapel. She had agreed to help serve food and pour tea and wash dishes and that kind of thing—maids' work, if you asked me. Were they planning to pay her? I wasn't cheeky enough to ask Mam. I imagined she'd agreed to do it without asking about money. And Liz wouldn't have thought to offer.

"No way," I replied. It was the last place I wanted to be, clearing away the plates of people who were crying fake tears over a girl they didn't even really know. I wasn't going to be anyone's servant.

"Okay. Well, you'll have to sort out your own tea. And don't bring anyone back to the house. And don't go out tonight, okay? It's not safe."

That night, the real funeral tea happened.

The Catholics call it a wake, don't they? We weren't religious, but *wake* seemed like a good word for that night. We had all been sleepwalking through the days since Greta died, and we knew that we needed something real, something loud and raw and almost grimy to wake us up.

Grief isn't quietly dabbing at wet eyes with an embroidered handkerchief. It isn't a whispered *I'm so sorry*. It's not a poem on the front of a sympathy card that someone else wrote.

It's *noisy*. It's *ugly*, full of swear words and bared teeth and the raw, bleeding violence of heartbreak.

The parents would have gone mad. The cops had told us not to go out without adults, of course, but we were used to blanking out their advice. Most adults thought that their children were good, mature, and sensible. And we were good—good at lying. They didn't know us.

The park was full, fuller than I'd ever seen it. People had been busy. It wasn't immediately obvious when you walked into the park that anything was happening at all—there was nothing happening in the part by the playground, or on the paths, but in the woods there were a lot of colored fairy lights hanging from the branches of the trees. Music was playing from a pair of speakers set up on some old tree stumps, and someone artistic had painted Greta's name in large, looping white letters down the trunk of the hugest tree in the park. It glowed in the dark like a ghost.

"If I die, this is how I want to go," said Ela. Stupid, insensitive thing to say, but no one objected. Our gang were all there, and Gwyn, Keira, and Ela had been up to Bryn Mawr to the official funeral tea for an hour. They sat with me and Dion on the damp, mossy ground, and Gwyn had swiped four bottles of prosecco from the cupboard at home—his mother had given up drinking because she had decided she was fat—and we passed them between us, swigging from the bottles.

"She'd have loved this," said Keira. "It's nuts, isn't it? She's really gone."

"That's what I keep obsessing over." Gwyn sighed. "Once you get over the shock, you start to think . . . she's gone. Forever. Like . . . her story's ended, you know what I mean? Now that the funeral is done . . . that's it. There's nothing else."

I didn't know whether anyone else noticed, but Ela gave a slight sigh. An impatient sigh. I looked up at her, surprised.

"What are you on about?" said Dion, rolling himself a smoke.

Gwyn shrugged before replying, "Well, we're gonna get old, aren't we? I mean, probably. We're gonna leave school, maybe go to college, get a job. Get married, have kids. All that shit. But her story's over."

I looked over at Ela again. Her mouth was pouty, turned out slightly as if she was waiting for a kiss. Was she annoyed about something?

"She'd have been brilliant at all that too," added Keira. "Passing exams, going to university. She'd have married someone amazing and had gorgeous, clever kids."

"Oh, for God's sake, give it a rest," said Ela, her voice hard as slate, and everyone turned to look at her.

◆ ◆ ◆

I haven't said much about Ela, have I?

I don't think anyone ever said much about Ela, because she was Greta's friend, and Greta always had everyone's attention. Since primary school, it had always been Greta, Keira, and Ela. Greta was the prettiest, the cleverest, the richest, and the most popular. Keira wasn't so good with her schoolwork, but she was interesting, in the way that people who lead damaged lives always are. People were slightly afraid of her. But Ela? Nothing. She lived on a nice estate with her parents and her brother. She wasn't poor but wasn't rich. I suppose she was quite pretty, petite and curvy and dark, but she was never going to be Greta.

There was something between her and Gwyn, who lived on the same estate as her, and their parents were friends. I could imagine them getting married one day and having two children exactly like themselves, buying a house on that exact estate that they lived on now, and living the same lives as their parents. It seemed to me a nice kind of life. Comfortingly boring.

I'd copped off with Ela myself a few times, and I think Dion had once last year too. She was like that, always wanting to end up with *someone* at the end of the night, even if they didn't care about her. She didn't care about them either. She was Gwyn's girl, really. We all knew it.

Once, about a year ago, I was skipping a PE lesson at school and was hiding out in the cloakroom when I found Ela sitting alone between the coats. It wasn't like her to be alone anywhere, and I knew that she had a PE lesson too.

"Didn't know you hate PE as much as I do," I said to her, a bit put out that she was there, because it meant I couldn't look through the coat pockets for some loose change or chocolate bars.

"The girls are doing gymnastics today. I'm rubbish at it."

"We're doing rugby. Stupid game."

There was a silence. I leaned against the wall, and she sat looking at her phone. It was awkward. The only times we'd been alone together before were when we'd been drunk and gotten together, but this was very different. I didn't know whether I had anything to say to her.

"I was going to do my geography homework here, but I don't think I can be arsed." I was bad at making conversation, but I felt I had to say *something*. "Have you done it? I'll get put on report if I don't hand it in this time."

"It's the shorts," she said, still looking at her phone, but I could tell by her voice that this was a big deal. It was sort of tight and small. She obviously wasn't talking about geography homework. "We have to wear gym shorts and T-shirts when we're doing gymnastics. That's why I don't like it."

"Right." I wasn't sure what she meant.

"I hate it."

"Why?"

She sighed and looked up at me, annoyed. "As if you don't know."

"Eh?"

"You don't have to try to be nice to me, you know. I'm not a charity case."

"*What?*"

She put her phone down and, to my horror, looked up at me with shining eyes. She was going to cry, and I had no idea what I'd done wrong. "What's up, El?"

"It's because the gym shorts show off my body, *okay*?" she said, her voice quaking now. I could see a quiver in her lower lip too. "I don't want anyone to see my horrible body."

I couldn't help it—I looked down at her, at her perfectly fine body, and wondered if I'd missed something. "I don't get it. You're not horrible."

"Yes I am!" She wiped her eyes with her sleeve and left a smear of mascara, like a scar, on the white cotton. "Everyone hates me!"

Afterward, I thought about all the things I should have told her, none of which I thought about at the time. That she was pretty and cool and fun, and that most of the girls in our year would do anything to be as popular as her. That I'd never heard anyone say anything unflattering or unkind about her, and that if it meant anything to her, and it really shouldn't, I thought she was good looking.

But I didn't think of any of this because I didn't know how to be kind without sounding creepy. I stood there, dumbfounded, and said nothing. Ela wept, and I fetched her some tissues and sat with her as she cried until she didn't.

"Don't you dare tell anyone I got upset," she said after blowing her nose. "Okay? I don't need anyone's pity."

"Fine," I replied—though, it stung that she seemed angry with me when I'd done nothing wrong. "But for the record, no one hates you. And you look . . . great."

She rolled her eyes and stood up. "You're never going to get it, being a boy." And off she went to wash her face and reapply her makeup, leaving her fresh perfume and a permanent memory of how insecure she was.

We never mentioned it again, but I remembered it sometimes when I looked at her laughing in class or walking down to the park arm in arm with Greta and Keira. We never copped off again—it would have felt wrong to me, as if I knew too much about her to take her lightly.

She was all right, Ela. I liked her. Above all, she wanted to please people, and that's why it was such a shock to see her losing her temper that night, the night of Greta's funeral.

◆ ◆ ◆

"Eh?" asked Keira, staring at Ela askance. Everyone was a bit drunk by now, and Dion was passing the smoke around the group.

"It's just stupid," replied Ela, her mouth a thin, tight line. "Look at these people! Look at them!" She pointed to a group of year-eight girls who were weeping as they talked about Greta. "They never knew her! They probably never even talked to her!"

"They're still allowed to have feelings," replied Keira, stunned at Ela's vehemence. "Does it matter?!"

"Yes, it does! You're all talking about her as if she was someone else! I've had enough of it. It's bullshit."

Gwyn shut his eyes, as if he'd known all along that this was coming—and I'd suspected it, too, but I'd never said anything. It was meant to be a secret, and I wasn't meant to know. "Don't listen to her, she's just pissed and upset . . ."

"Don't even start with all that," Ela bit back, an expression on her face I'd never seen before. "You, especially. We all know why *you're* so upset."

"Am I missing something here?" asked Keira, looking from one face to the other.

Ela stumbled onto her feet. She was thoroughly, properly drunk, and she took a while to find her balance. "We pretend she was so bloody perfect, but she treated us all like shit, in different ways. And it's so typical that this is happening now!" She waved her hands about, her lazy eyes looking at the fairy lights and the paint and the people, all celebrating the life of Greta. "Even when she dies, she manages to look perfect. She died before she could fail at anything. We'll all live long enough to fuck things up. We can't win." She turned and swayed her way toward the path leading to the village. If she'd been allowed to leave, everything would have been so different. Everyone would have judged Ela as the drunk girl who was jealous of her pretty, dead friend who was now turned to ash, the smoke of her burning body having drifted across Bangor and out to sea hours ago.

But Keira wasn't going to let her go. Of course she wasn't. Although Greta had gone, Keira was her best friend, and she was going to stand up for her. She leaped to her feet and stared at Ela, her face flashing with rage.

"What the hell's wrong with you? She's been killed! Her funeral was today, for fuck's sake!"

Ela turned back to face us. "What's wrong with me?" she asked slowly, sarcastically, another rhetorical question. "Why don't you ask *him* where he was on the night Greta was killed?" She pointed at Gwyn. "Because the last I saw, they were holding hands and heading into the trees."

CHAPTER 7

There were voices in our house the next morning.

I say morning. It had been a late, late night, and I hadn't gotten home until about two—it was never going to be an early one after everything that happened, after all the prosecco and vodka. Things had gone a bit mad. Gwyn spent the rest of the night crying and admitted that he and Greta had copped off on the night she died. "I wanted to tell you, but I didn't want to get the blame for stuff I didn't do. She went off on her own afterward . . . you know what it's like . . ." He was heartbroken, and of course we all believed him. He wouldn't have harmed Greta. Not him. He was too nice. The relief he felt on being believed turned into floods of tears at finally being able to talk about his secret. He wept until his face swelled up and became distorted and he looked like someone else. "I couldn't tell anyone in case they thought . . ."

I pretended that all this was news to me.

It was probably after lunchtime when I woke up, my mouth parched after last night's drinking and the taste of old smoke thick on my tongue. I was still in my clothes, including my coat, and my phone had run out of battery. I must have been really drunk.

I got up to go to the bathroom. I could hear voices but assumed Mam was doing the ironing in front of the TV again.

I was brushing the taste of last night from my teeth when I realized that the voices weren't from the television—Mam was talking to someone. I knew that voice.

Shit. DCI Davies. DCI Call Me Karen, the small woman who was desperate for us to believe that she understood us. That woman who was so clever that she became stupid. She was never ever going to catch the killer.

Why was she sniffing around us the day after the funeral?

I opened the door of the bathroom and stepped out slowly and quietly. Our house was tiny, so I could hear their conversation from the landing. I sat on the top step silently, listening.

Bloody hell.

Mam was crying.

"Look, I know this is difficult for you." Mam cleared her throat of her tears, and DCI Karen went on. "But we just have to establish the facts. Of course we've seen Kelvin Pugh's phone, so we know about the messages—but could you tell us about it? In your own words?"

Mam sniffed. My fists became tighter and tighter.

What bloody messages?

"I knew him from school. Kelvin. And Liz, of course—I knew them both, but they wouldn't have remembered me. He didn't seem to, anyway, when I started working for them. He was kind at first. Really kind. I liked him, you know—well, you've met him. He's sweet. Comes across a bit . . . I don't know . . . innocent. Naive. And whatever happened, he doesn't deserve what happened. Not at all."

I thought about Kelvin. Greta's father.

"How do you mean *kind*?"

"He'd make me nice coffees when I'd go there to clean. They've got one of those posh coffee machines, you know—he said he liked making them. He'd make me a latte after I'd done the cleaning, and then he'd sit down for a chat. People don't usually do that with the cleaning lady, you know—we're not treated as friends. Of course Liz was always out at work."

"Did you have a sexual relationship with him, Miss Jones?"

Jesus Christ.

"No. But I *did* fancy him at one point. He gave me attention! And I had no one else. I've had no one else for years. You forget what it's like to have someone look at you in that way—it makes you feel alive again. When you're older, you become so . . . invisible. *You're* young and pretty—you wouldn't get it."

Mam fancied Greta's dad? He made her some horrible posh coffees? I tried to imagine them sitting together in the huge kitchen in Bryn Mawr, but I couldn't quite manage to create the picture in my head. The pieces didn't fit.

"What would you two talk about?"

"Everything. I'd tell him when things were hard. And sometimes . . . sometimes he'd say something similar. Say that he and Liz weren't getting on. That their marriage wouldn't last much longer. That's when I started thinking that there was something . . . well. That he wanted me."

I heard Mam's soft sigh and found my heart torn between feelings of sympathy and disgust. Had she really thought that a rich, posh man like Kelvin Pugh was going to leave his wife for a woman like her?

"Then one day . . . shit, it was nothing, really . . . we were drinking our coffees, and he was saying how Liz barely even looked at him anymore. And he moved his foot under the table to touch mine. Just a tiny bit. And I knew then that he wanted more."

For some reason, that one movement—Kelvin's foot touching my mother's under the table—made me feel like punching something. That bastard. He'd taken advantage of my mam.

"But nothing happened?"

"I pulled back. I don't know why. I thought he was kind and good looking and all that, but it felt odd that he was paying me to clean his house, and if we . . . you know . . . he'd kind of be paying me for that, wouldn't he? Plus, he'd give me bonuses sometimes, without saying anything. There'd be extra money in my wage envelope. And he'd do that after just a chat, so it felt . . . I don't know. Weird."

"I understand. Did he try again?"

"Something changed after that. They didn't want me to clean so often, and they made sure that I went over when Liz wasn't out working. I don't know why. But something was different. I guess he felt rejected."

There was a silence, and then a different voice. A man. There must be another police officer down there.

"We've spoken to Mr. Pugh after searching through his phone. He said that *you* were the one who moved your foot to touch his and that *you* had been the one flirting."

I heard Mam's deep breath—she was shocked, unprepared for this. "Honest to God, I never! I wouldn't have! It's been years since I flirted with anyone, and I'd never dare to do it with a man who was my boss. I . . . I don't know what to tell you. It's just not me, to do that."

"We're only repeating what they said." DCI Karen's voice was kinder, softer. They had the good-cop–bad-cop routine all worked out. It was so bloody obvious. I wondered if it came naturally to them or if they'd decided on the way here who would take which role.

"You don't suspect me of anything, do you?" Mam asked in a weak voice.

"We're just trying to establish all the facts about Greta's homelife," said the policeman. "Now, the text messages . . ."

"They were nothing to begin with. Kelvin thanking me for the cleaning job I'd done. Telling me how much he appreciated me. Then texts asking if I was okay, and then another if I didn't reply straight away. He'd put kisses at the end of every message. I'd reply, but I tried to be as professional as I could. Nothing personal. No kisses. But then he'd text saying I could phone him anytime, that he would come over whenever I wanted, night or day. For a chat, or anything."

Or anything. That fucking bastard.

"Did you call him? Did he ever come here?"

"No, never. I didn't like the attention. I used to think he was sweet, but he was more like a dirty old man. A creep, you know? Probably harmless, but creepy."

"Yes."

"Those things are so close, don't you think? Being kind and being creepy."

"But you carried on cleaning for them. Why? If you felt so uncomfortable?" The policeman's voice was hard edged, the consonants clipped, and the question angered me. Only a man who had always had money would ever ask such a thing.

"I needed the cash," Mam replied quietly, as if she was ashamed. "I had no choice."

"Mrs. Jones, did you ever witness any arguments between Mr. and Mrs. Pugh? Or Greta, perhaps?" DCI Karen asked kindly.

"No. They were busy—I didn't see them together that often. And Greta was always at school."

"Thank you, Miss Jones. You've been a great help." I heard the sofa springs creaking; that meant they were about to leave. I considered moving from my spot on the top step in order to hide, but what would be the point? They weren't here for me. So I sat there and saw them coming from the living room and toward the front door. They didn't notice I was there until I spoke.

"Mam's not weak, you know." The three of them looked up at me. Mam shook her head, upset that I had heard it all. "You think she's weak, going back there to clean when Greta's dad was perving on her."

"We don't think that." DCI Karen gave me the kind of smile you'd give a six-year-old when you're trying to get them to behave. "You're Shane, aren't you?"

"You've got to realize what kind of man he is."

"Shane, stop," Mam pleaded, not wanting any of this.

"What kind of man puts his employee in that situation? Flirting and texting and trying it on, knowing that Mam *had* to go to his house, *had* to spend time with him? What do you think about a man who does that?"

◆ ◆ ◆

Mam and I didn't talk about the things I'd heard. I knew that none of it was her fault, but for some reason, I couldn't help but feel angry at her. We'd been quiet since the police left, but when she called out, "I'm going," I yelled, "Okay, take care!" And then we both knew that we were okay.

Everyone has their secrets. I didn't know who Mam was when she wasn't with me. She didn't know me either, and yet she was the one who knew me best.

I couldn't be bothered going out—I was still hungover. But when I plugged the charger into my phone and it came to life, I saw that Gwyn had been texting all morning; his name appeared over and over again, each message more desperate than the last. He was worried about what Ela had revealed the night before. I could read the panic in his messages, and I replied to the most recent one.

Come over plz. I'm goin off my head.

Calm down Gwyn.

I dnt no if I shld tel the cops.

Hang on. I'll be there at half past. Twat.

No one else was home at Gwyn's house, which was a shame because Gwyn's mother was one of the kindest women I knew. She always spoke to me as if I was an adult, and she'd ask about Mam and how school was and what I was doing with myself these days. Gwyn's dad was kind, too, and even his little sister was okay. Gwyn was lucky.

"What the hell am I gonna do?" he asked me once he'd fetched us each a can of Coke. We were sitting in his back garden, where he'd been lounging on a towel all morning, pretending to study. I hadn't done any homework for ages, but I don't think his copies of *An Inspector Calls* and *Of Mice and Men* had been looked at today either. We used them as coasters.

"You do nothing, you idiot," I replied. "Keep your mouth shut. Anyway, you have nothing to say! Yes, you copped off with Greta, but you didn't kill her."

"Of course I didn't. But I should have just told them from the start. I just panicked."

"And you're still panicking. Stop thinking about it. It's done."

"But surely they must know that she'd . . . been with someone? Before she died?"

"I don't know. If you were safe . . . Were you safe?"

"Yes, but . . ."

"There you go, then! They've already said that she wasn't sexually attacked . . ."

"I never attacked her!"

"I know that, don't I, you dick. Stop worrying."

"I can't. It's driving me nuts. I think I'd better just come clean . . ."

"Just let me think."

"D'you know . . . this is really crap, but before I knew what had happened to Greta . . . I couldn't wait to tell you . . ." Gwyn shook his head as I finished off my can of Coke and started on his. It was soothing my hangover.

"What about?"

"That I'd pulled Greta! I'd planned to invite you and Dion over; then I'd tell you face to face so that I could see your expressions when I told you. I was so bloody proud of myself!" He looked up to see my reaction. "Is that pathetic?"

"Of course not. I'd have been the same."

Gwyn sighed with relief. "You're not just saying that?"

"No. She was gorgeous. And she never copped off with boys from school, so I'd have bragged about it too."

Something nagged at the back of my mind.

Why *had* Greta been with Gwyn? It just wasn't like her. Especially as she'd known that Ela adored him. And Gwyn wasn't one of the most handsome or popular boys at school. Yes, Greta had been drunk . . . but not that drunk.

A memory worked its way into my mind, as sharp as a splinter, as Greta's soft voice filled my head.

Of her, in the sun, lying in Cae Du field in a crop top and shorts, her belly nut brown and smooth. She was wearing sunglasses with reflective lenses, and I didn't like looking at her because I could see myself. She had one brown freckle just to the left of her belly button.

"God, it's lovely here." Her voice was low and soft edged, as if she'd just woken up.

"Yeah. This is my favorite place, I think." I'd never been here without Greta. It was a long, narrow field, with a drystone wall on one side and a slate-slab fence on the other. It looked out over the quarry and the mountains, but it wasn't really a field—more of a dead space between places.

"I prefer the quarry," said Greta, looking at it across the valley. The slates were looking particularly bright that day, vividly purple, but the quarry was still just a hole in the earth. As if someone had gone there chasing buried treasure but had given up looking when halfway through the mountain.

"I don't like the quarry. It's just . . . all broken up."

"Maybe that's why I like it." Greta's lips curled into a tiny ghost of a smile. "There are so many mountains. The really special one is the only one with its heart taken out."

◆ ◆ ◆

"When did you last see her?" I asked Gwyn, trying to rid my mind of that one brown freckle on Greta's belly. He had tried to explain everything the night before, but he'd been drunk and upset and mumbling, and I'd been too wasted to listen.

"I wanted to walk back to you lot with her, but she didn't want to. She said she was meeting someone else by the gate, and I was a bit pissed off about it. I felt like she was embarrassed of me. So I let her go." The gate was on the path leading to the quarry.

"She didn't say who she was meeting?"

"No. You know what she was like, Shane. You always knew that you didn't know the half of it with Greta." But I hadn't known that everyone felt like that about Greta, not just me. I hadn't realized until she was gone.

I stayed with Gwyn for hours, chatting about Greta and school and football and everything. He needed empty talking, and he was my friend. It felt so normal for a while.

"I wonder if they killed her with a slate, or was there something else?"

"Dunno. Hey, did you hear that Arsenal are trying to sign a new striker from Inter Milan?"

Anyone would have thought we were cold hearted, but you don't know how real life breaks into conversations when you're living through a tragedy. We understood one another.

When Gwyn's parents and sister came home, we were pretending to study. I don't know if they were bothered—Gwyn's mother, especially, seemed happy that he was talking to someone after Greta's death. Of course she didn't know that her darling little boy had ground his body into Greta's against a tree on the night she died.

Before I left, I asked Gwyn if he had heard from Ela since last night.

"Nothing," he replied. "She's annoyed. But I didn't do anything wrong . . . She's not my girlfriend, is she? So I didn't cheat."

"She really likes you, you know. And it'd be a good idea to get on her good side now. You don't want her blabbing."

"D'you think she would?"

"Well, yeah, I do, to be honest. She's jealous of Greta, even now. Why don't you ask her out?"

"Be her boyfriend, like?"

"Yeah. D'you want to?"

"I dunno. Yeah, maybe. She's a nice girl. Isn't she?"

"Yeah, she's all right. You know where you are with Ela." I didn't think about it at the time, but looking back, I wonder if what I really meant was that she was boring. And I wondered, did I actually know what kind of girl she was? Was she really a nice girl, even though she was mad with jealousy about her friend who was beaten to death and left, alone and bleeding?

CHAPTER 8

After she'd visited Mam in our home, I hated seeing DCI Call Me Karen at school.

And it felt like she was there all the time. Strolling down the corridor in one of her smart suits or chatting to one of the teachers with that head-tilted, faux-sympathetic nod that she had. I didn't think it was right that there were so many cops in the school. It didn't make anyone feel safer. It made us feel as though we needed protecting.

Everyone in our class was individually questioned, of course. On our first day back at school after the murder, the police took each of us to one side and fired questions at us—Where were we on Saturday night? Who was Greta with? Was there anything that they should know? It was a cold, quick-fire interview of desperation. But then after a week, they came round once more, wanted to talk to us all again, take their time with us. We were expecting that much. Keira and Ela, as Greta's best friends, were questioned a few times, at school and at home.

"What do they want to know?" Gwyn asked when we were all sitting around the same lunch table one day. It was almost our turn to be questioned. We'd had letters sent home, saying that we could have a parent present when we were talking to the police officers, and telling us when that would be. Most people had their mothers with them. Gwyn was having both his parents with him. Of course I didn't want Mam there, and I don't think that she particularly wanted to come either.

"It's not formal," Keira said casually, picking at her sandwich. "They ask about that night, but then they want to know about Greta and what she was really like."

"They asked me about who she fancied, that kind of thing," Ela said, pulling a face. "You'd have thought we were about twelve, the way they talked about crushes and that sort of thing." I said nothing as I tucked into my cheese sandwich, but I thought it was an odd thing to say, as if having crushes and fancying people were childish. Ela was strange that way. When she tried to appear adult, it made her seem younger, like a little girl playing grown up. I wondered how Gwyn could be attracted to her when she was so naive, so easy to read.

My turn to be questioned came one afternoon when I should have been in a geography lesson. I stood outside one of the school offices, waiting to be called in, wondering if other people could hear my heart thumping or if it was just me.

"Come on in, Shane."

I pushed open the door and tried to hide my surprise. This had always been a dull, gray office, somewhere people came to get told off or to wait for their parents when they were ill and had to go home. But the mold-colored table and uncomfortable plastic chairs had been replaced with a long, low wine-colored sofa, a few easy chairs, and a coffee table with a vase of fresh flowers on it and a box of tissues should anyone burst into tears.

DCI Call Me Karen was sitting on one of the chairs, and in the other chair was a young plainclothes police officer, a handsome man who looked like he might be a footballer or a soap actor or someone who modeled jeans for a living. He stood up straight away, a kind, open smile on his face, and offered me his hand. I shook it, of course—it would have been rude not to. But there was something a little bit patronizing about a grown man in a position of power wanting to shake hands with me. He was trying to make me think that we were equals.

I didn't trust him.

"I'm Jake. I'm a police officer, and I'm here to help Karen with her inquiries."

He was a police officer. Of course I didn't trust him.

"All right, Shane? Take a seat." Karen smiled at me, but it was awkward—the last time we'd spoken had been at home when she came to talk to Mam. I didn't like the fact that she'd been in my house with my things. That she knew stuff about my mother, things that felt like secrets. She knew about the thoughts that Mam had had about Kelvin, and she had probably, like me, imagined the thickness of the air in the kitchen when Mam went to clean Bryn Mawr, the way that oxygen seems weighted when people want to touch one another.

She probably hadn't imagined it as much as I had. Probably hadn't lain awake at night, turning the horror of it over and over in her head.

Sometimes I felt that the idea of my mother being attracted to such a man was more terrible to me than the murder of Greta.

I swallowed the thought away and sat down on the sofa. It even had throw pillows with cutesy pictures of sheep on them, for God's sake.

"A bit of a change, isn't it?" said Jake, sitting back down. "Not quite as miserable as it was before."

"I wanted to create a space that made pupils feel comfortable . . . somewhere that doesn't feel like school," Call Me Karen said in a voice that tried to sound soft.

"Looks a bit like a therapist's office," I ventured, before correcting myself. "Like I imagine one looks like, anyway. Like they look on the telly." Shit. I was stuttering already, as if I was trying to hide something.

"That is *exactly* what I said!" Jake grinned. "Isn't it?" he asked Karen.

"Yes. Yes, you did." And she gave a small smile too. I wondered whether they'd discussed beforehand how much smiling was appropriate, given the circumstances. I wondered if Jake had rehearsed his persona before he came to work in the morning or whether he'd been on a course that taught him how to speak to young people so that they would open up. He'd probably have a certificate.

"You know why we're here, Shane," said Karen, her face suddenly gray and serious. "And we know that you and Greta were friends."

Something swirled in my stomach. How much did they know?

Don't panic, I thought. *They know nothing. You're a better actor than they are.*

"Yes," I replied, carefully edging my voice with a hint of sadness.

"There were a group of you, weren't there? You'd sometimes meet up on nights out. Have lunch together once a week. Would you say that you and Greta were close?"

I'd practiced my answers. Only someone with something to hide would reply negatively to that question—everyone wanted to feel close to the popular dead girl, and I had to be just like them. "Yes. She was lovely."

The police officers nodded sympathetically. Jake gave me a sad smile.

"What did you like to talk about?" he asked.

"Well, homework and things like that." I swallowed, hoping that I looked as if I was trying to hide distress. "And sometimes, she stole my sweets. I mean, I let her. We laughed about it. I didn't mind."

Karen looked down at the notepad in her lap, but not before I saw it in her eyes—a flicker of disappointment. Perfect. I'd managed to sound like I was on the periphery of Greta's life, didn't really know her that well at all.

"Did you ever . . . was there ever anything between you and Greta? Romantically?" Karen asked the question as though she already knew the answer.

I shook my head, tried to look embarrassed. I shifted in my seat a bit, like people do when they're uncomfortable with the conversation. "No. She was never really like that with anyone. Not that I knew of, anyway."

"Did you ever hear of anyone at all? Any boys—men—that she might have gone out with, or maybe copped off with?" asked Jake.

I managed to steel myself enough to catch his eye and shake my head.

"Not even at parties."

"And was there anyone who didn't get on with Greta? Anyone she'd have argued with, or someone who might have been jealous of her?"

"No, no, she wasn't the arguing type. There was never any drama." I cleared my throat. "Although, yeah, loads of people would have been jealous of her, I suppose. She had everything going for her, didn't she. She was beautiful and clever and minted . . . but she wasn't braggy."

Call Me Karen nodded, scribbled down something in her notebook—it might even have been a cross, indicating that I knew nothing.

"Tell me about that night." Jake leaned in a bit closer as if he was a friend asking me to tell him the gossip. "The night she died."

"We were all out in the park. There was a party." I looked down at my hands, as if recounting the story was difficult. "Everyone was there."

"Drinking?" asked Karen, which was stupid because she already knew the answer. I nodded.

"Yeah, drinking, and smoking weed."

Karen nodded, her eyebrows slightly raised as if she was impressed that someone had admitted it.

Shit. Had I said too much? I had to remind them that I was just a schoolkid, dumb and scared. "You won't tell my mam, will you?"

Jake wore his sad smile again. "Don't worry about any of that, mate. Go on." Thank God for that. They were buying my act.

"It was like any other party. It wasn't wild or anything."

"And did you see Greta?"

I nodded vigorously. "Yes, we hung around with the rest of our mates for a bit. She was in a good mood."

"What was she talking about?" Karen scribbled nonstop in her notebook.

"She was talking for a bit about an essay that was meant to be in the next Monday. . . and then she was talking to Keira about what she'd bought that day . . . I think she'd been shopping with her parents."

"Greta was staying at Keira's house that night, wasn't she?" I nodded. "And yet, Keira didn't raise the alarm when Greta didn't come
home. Why do you think that was?"

"Well . . . Greta might have been really drunk and stayed at someone else's house. And sometimes people fall asleep in the woods and
don't wake up until dawn."

"It wouldn't have been because maybe Greta was meeting a man?"
Karen shot out the question, her tone a little sharp, thinking she'd take
me by surprise. So I pretended to be surprised.

"I don't think so! No . . . I mean, people get off with one another,
but we all still live with our parents. We've got nowhere we can go
to . . . you know."

Call Me Karen and Jake questioned me for a long time, but once
I started answering them, it felt easy to lie. I just had to pretend to
be somebody else, that's all. To be who they thought I was. And so I
behaved like I was a bit of a loser, a bit stupid, a bit in awe of the fact
that I had a connection to a famous dead girl. They would have thought
that, although, yes, I had been in the same friend group as Greta, we
weren't really friends—I was probably annoying to her, a hanger-on.
To the police, I was nothing but another dead end, with no possible
connection or explanation as to why someone had killed Greta.

"Just one last thing," said Karen after they had been listening to me
for half an hour. "Shane, I met you at your home, didn't I? When I came
to talk about your mother's relationship with Greta's father?"

I'd expected this line of questioning, too, but it still made me
uncomfortable. I hadn't been acting when she'd turned up at my home.
She'd seen a glimpse of the real me, and I didn't want that happening
again.

"Yes."

"And you seemed quite angry."

She let the silence stretch on between us. I could hear someone
walking down the corridor outside, someone in heels click-clacking
between classrooms like a clock keeping time.

"I was angry."

Jake nodded like he understood perfectly. "Can you explain why?"

I nodded back at him, as if I didn't understand his game, as if he'd reeled me in to trusting him. "I heard about Kelvin trying it on with my mam. I didn't like it."

"Why was that, d'you think?" asked Karen, and I dared to look up at her as if she was stupid.

"Because he's *married*! And because she's their cleaner . . . It's just weird, isn't it?"

They weren't allowed to agree with me, of course. But I knew that they did. And I knew that I didn't want them thinking that I was as clever as I was. It was easier for them to think that I had reacted out of spite or out of weird jealousy after having my mother to myself for all these years.

"You don't like Kelvin, do you?" asked Karen.

"Not really. It's horrible what happened to Greta. He never deserved that. But I don't think he's a nice man, because he made my mam feel uncomfortable."

"And what did you think of him before Greta died? Before you found out about the advances he'd made on your mother?"

I shook my head. "I didn't really know him. I think Greta had to pretend she wasn't going out, didn't have any friends that were boys, that sort of thing. But maybe that's what dads are like with their daughters." This, I knew, was bullshit, but it suited the character I was playing to say it. "I've seen him around, of course. He's a big farmer type. I never really thought about him before."

Not only had I thought about him many, many times before, but I'd made mental lists of ways to kill him—poison, a fall down the mountain, an axe to the head. But the police didn't need to know that.

"Thanks, mate," said Jake as I got up to leave the room, our interview over. "If you think of anything that might be of use to us, give us a shout, yeah?" I nodded and wondered if the course he'd been on taught people how to talk like young people too. Call Me Karen gave me a tight smile and thanked me, and I left knowing that to them I was clueless and a bit dumb and knew nothing about what had happened to Greta.

◆ ◆ ◆

Adults spend so much of their time manipulating young people.

Particularly parents, teachers, and cops. I wondered if they ever thought about it, if they ever acknowledged that they were doing it, and if it was healthy or respectful.

I was lucky. Mam wasn't like that. But most of my friends had felt that terrible sinking feeling of shame when a school report made their mam or dad feel *not angry, but disappointed.* Most of them carried around the weight of expectation—that they had to be clever or creative or sporty or excellent at something or else their parents would feel let down. They wanted to feel good enough for their parents. And I wondered how that kind of feeling might work if it was *not* about a parent and child, but about two friends or a husband and wife. Would it not feel unkind, unfair, or manipulative for a husband to say to a wife after a bad test score—*I'm not angry with you; I'm just disappointed?*

Why did being a parent make it okay?

And teachers, too, with their cultlike belief that school was the only path to success, without ever being able to give an adequate definition of success. Their insistence on the importance of passing English and science and math exams, their unfaltering faith in the fact that we *needed* to know how to work out percentages, explain the conservation and the transfer of energy in physics, and memorize the prologue to *Romeo and Juliet* in order to secure our future happiness. Teachers who disappeared by the time those at the top of the class graduated from university with tens of thousands of pounds of debt and no jobs except for serving at the drive-through burger place or cleaning hotels, while the kids from their class at school who were builders and electricians and plumbers already owned their own homes and could afford holidays abroad. I wondered what people would think if that was the relationship between friends and not teacher and pupil. Would it not feel wrong for a friend to lie to you about which path would bring you happiness, knowing full well that you were planning your life based on that lie?

Why did being a teacher make it okay?

The police, or at least the ones I knew, tried to keep the peace by using fear. They were absent when we needed them, taking over an hour to arrive when called to a domestic where a man dosed up on cocaine was holding his wife at knifepoint, or simply nodding and doing nothing when a group of women made complaints that one of the regulars in their local pub was filming up their miniskirts and pushing his phone camera into their cleavage. Yet when someone from the estate was driving his mother to the hospital at four miles an hour over the limit, they were there, handing out a fine. When one of Mam's school friends was caught growing the cannabis that she smoked to help ease the pain of her gnawing, crippling arthritis, they arrested her and charged her, and she was given a suspended sentence and a fine, which she was paying in installments for five years. She could barely stand straight in the dock. Would it be acceptable in any other circumstance for someone to keep you safe by making you fear them? What if a man did that to his new girlfriend? Ignored the threats made toward her but made sure that she paid dearly for any wrongdoing? We'd be calling it abuse.

Why did being a police officer make it okay?

And I knew, even then more than ever, that every question and interview about Greta was tinged with manipulation. When they asked me what she was like, they also wanted to know what *I* was like. When they asked me about the conversations I'd had with her, about her hobbies, about her friends, their dearest hope was that I'd slip up and say something incriminating about myself. That was all they wanted, for someone to mess up and make themselves seem suspicious. Then they could arrest and charge, and we'd all go back to pretending that they cared about the safety and well-being of people.

They didn't want justice. They wanted to win in court.

So when Jake shook my hand and smiled at me, when he called me *mate* and nodded in sympathy and behaved as if he truly liked me, I knew that it wasn't sincere. He'd learned how to pretend to be friends with people like me because it served a purpose for him. I didn't trust him, and I didn't trust Call Me Karen, and I didn't know anyone else who did either.

"She looks nervous," Keira said a few days later. We had a PE lesson, and we were meant to be running cross-country. Dion and Gwyn had raced ahead across the field and toward the hill, Gwyn because he was competitive enough to care and Dion just because running felt like it released something that was always bubbling inside him. The other boys, the sporty ones, had form and technique to their running, but Dion, who always ran as if someone was chasing him down, was faster than them all.

I wasn't running for anyone. Keira, Ela, and I had fallen into step together as we walked the path as slowly as we could get away with, and Call Me Karen was standing beside Miss Rees, the PE teacher, who had stationed herself at the top of the netball court, where she could have a good look at the runners.

Keira was right. Karen *did* look nervous. She was the same as usual in that she was neat and tidy, her movements boxy and controlled, but she was standing at an angle to Miss Rees, and we could see her fists tightening and loosening.

"I wonder what she wants with Miss Rees," I said.

"Well, she knew Greta pretty well, didn't she. Netball team, girls' football team," replied Ela, who was also on both of those teams and was competitive when she was part of a team. I wondered whether it had ever annoyed her that Greta was a better sportswoman than her. "She shouldn't have to interview her out here, though. Not in the middle of a lesson!"

"She's getting desperate," said Keira flatly. "Interviewing people twice, hanging around the school, not quite knowing what to do now that there aren't any leads. She's stressed that she hasn't caught the bad guy yet."

"Or bad woman," I corrected her absentmindedly.

"Unlikely, statistically."

"They'll have a profile of the killer, won't they?" asked Ela. "So they'll be looking for a specific type of person."

"Yeah," I agreed. "White man, between eighteen and . . . I dunno . . . fifty? Do old people become murderers?"

"I'd say sixty," said Keira. "He'll be charming and popular."

"I don't think so," I disagreed, watching Dion disappear in a whizzing black line over the brow of the hill. The rest of the class wheezed their way behind him. "He'll be a social outcast, a bit of a weirdo. Never quite fit in."

"No." Keira and Ela spoke together, united in their opinion. Ela was twisting the bottom of her ponytail around her fist, like a thick black snake. Her eyes were still on Call Me Karen.

"Keira's right. Charming, popular. He'll have lots of friends."

I looked at Ela. Under her makeup, her skin was maybe paler than it might have been, her eyes a little tired. I realized that I hadn't considered her grief in the same way as I had for Keira, and that was because I liked Keira so much more and because I considered Keira to be so much more astute and straightforward than Ela.

"How do you know this stuff?" I asked them.

"It's not the weirdos you have to worry about," replied Ela, still twisting her hair in her fist, still staring at Karen. "It's the ones that seem normal."

We stood by the gym wall and watched Karen marching back down to school, a certain stiffness in her movements, her short dark hair slicked back behind her ears. At the other side of the school grounds, Miss Rees watched her, too, her hands on her hips as if she was assessing her for PE.

I wondered what the normal-seeming men had done to Ela and Keira.

And as we started walking again, the girls chatting about Karen and how she always wore the same type of thing and smiled the same kind of smile, I wondered if I was one of those normal men. One of those who seemed okay and friendly and nice but was hiding a rotten core, a bitterness.

I knew that I unfairly judged Ela, for instance.

Yes, she was annoying, and she was competitive, and she was snobbish and a bit judgmental, and she probably unfairly judged me too. But I didn't like her in the same way as I liked Greta and Keira, and the main reason was because of the way she looked.

She was stunning.

Not in the same way as Greta. Ela wasn't going to be beautiful forever, and she was attractive in an obvious way, with the type of face and body that pervy men enjoyed. That wasn't her fault, of course, but I couldn't help the fact that I had a bit of an aversion to it. Her black hair was perfect, every day, all the time. Her clothes were carefully selected to show off the curves of her body, but while not looking cheap or gratuitous. And her makeup annoyed me most of all—thick and glutinous over her skin, the shade slightly too pale for her natural skin tone. Her lips were always lined with brown and always shone as if they were wet, and her eyebrows were perfect arches, not a stray hair to be seen anywhere, like the outstretched wings of a vulture above her eyes. I had no idea what she really looked like because, since year eight, she'd been wearing this thick layer of paint on her face every single day.

It annoyed me. I didn't want to admit it to myself, but it was true— her insecurity got on my nerves, her neediness, the lengths she went to in order to look pretty. Although I knew it wasn't true, a part of me thought she must be shallow, a bit stupid, a bit ridiculous to curate herself so perfectly all the time. Even after her best mate was murdered. Even then, she managed to set her false eyelashes absolutely perfectly above her eyes.

Greta hadn't been like that.

Yes, she wore makeup and nice clothes that suited her, but she didn't hide herself behind them. Sometimes after PE lessons, she wouldn't bother with makeup at all. I suppose she was prettier than Ela and could get away with more.

I suppose Ela knew that. I suppose it was difficult for her, trying so hard but never being the prettiest in the class. I suppose she hated Greta for it sometimes.

As I walked behind Ela and Keira, I realized that Ela was probably the most attractive girl in our year now. I was sure that she'd thought about it. It would have been one of the first thoughts in her head, after the shock of finding out that Greta was gone. She would have stood in the mirror, redoing her mascara after all the weeping, and she would have met her own eyes and stared at herself, at the beautiful, painted face that stared back at her.

I followed Keira and Ela around the whole track and back to school, only occasionally chatting with them, mostly half listening to their conversation about Karen and school and Greta. And all the time, I thought about how I couldn't bring myself to like Ela and wondered if that meant that I was one of those men, judgmental and cruel and hiding in plain sight.

CHAPTER 9

I didn't like men.

Lots of people didn't. But it was particularly unfortunate for me because I was becoming one. And in the way lads wait for the signs of their impending adulthood impatiently, hoping for hair on their legs and for their voices to drop into a low, velvety growl, I didn't know how to feel about these things. I wanted to be like the others, of course, but I didn't want to be like the others at all, not if we were all to become men. What kind of ambition was that?

I could never bring myself to experiment with the thick, bristly hairs that grew out of my chin and upper lip. When the hairs had started appearing on Dion and Gwyn and the others a few years before, they attempted the occasional pathetic mustache and sideburns, but I had shaved my face every single morning since the hairs started to come. I kept a disgusted eye on my growth and bodily changes, like the way my sweat started to smell like man sweat, gathering thickly in the folds of my T-shirts.

One day when I was fourteen, I caught my reflection in the mirror at the bottom of the stairs and thought to myself, *The little boy has gone. Am I going to be bad now?* And I felt, even at the time, that I was being childish and silly, that of course not all men were bad and cruel and careless of the feelings of others. But then, why didn't I know any good ones? Why were so many of them—so many of *us*—so disappointing?

I didn't like the male teachers at school and tried to keep out of their way, saying nothing in their classes, trying to disappear into the crowd. Not that I was much different with the female teachers—though, I felt myself relax a bit more with them and would even allow myself to enjoy some lessons.

Don't get me wrong. I knew that not all men were awful and that there were some good ones out there. There were men who were nothing like my dad and granddad, nothing like Kelvin Pugh and his boorish, arrogant, moneyed friends, the ones who drove about in their new pickup trucks, high above the other drivers on the road, the ones who came back from lads' trips to see the rugby, with nothing but bleary eyes and a strangled gaggle of rumors. They somehow managed to make money seem filthy and polluting. Every time I smelled coins on my fingers—that metallic, bloodlike tang—I imagined that was how Kelvin and his friends smelled underneath their clothes, like blood and rust.

Even the good men seemed just okay. I suppose that they were the majority and that they were only good because they weren't awful like my dad or Kelvin. I'd been in the homes of my friends and had silently, secretly observed what it was like to have a dad at home, parents that chose to be together. People like Gwyn's parents. They seemed to be actively *happy* with one another, even though they'd been together since school. When Gwyn and I were playing on the console or listening to music, I could hear them chatting away in the kitchen, laughing every so often at one another's jokes. Once when I was leaving to go home, I passed by the kitchen, where Gwyn's mam was stirring something in a big pot on the stove, his dad was putting away the dishes from the dishwasher, and the little speaker in the corner was blasting out "Linger" by the Cranberries, and they were both singing along to it. They weren't making a fuss or giggling or messing around; it's just that they were singing together, naturally, with him taking the low harmony and her taking the higher notes. His dad saw me leaving and smiled. "You off home, Shane?" And after that, whenever I thought about love and romance and being truly happy with another person, I thought of them, singing together in the kitchen.

He was a nice man. Dependable. He'd go to work in the morning and come home in the evening, and he'd put the dishes in the dishwasher every night and read Gwyn's sister a bedtime story before she slept. He'd sometimes take Gwyn to football matches at Anfield as a treat, and he'd always buy flowers for his wife on Valentine's Day and would tell her that she looked gorgeous even when she didn't. He was the kind of man women dream of.

But he probably didn't know how much milk was left in the fridge or if he needed to stop at the shop on the way home from work to buy bread. He didn't know which day his children did PE at school and needed a clean uniform, and he didn't know about their medical appointments, or their shoe size, or what reading level his daughter was on. He didn't have to plan every dinner at their home, trying to cook something healthy that everyone would eat and that wouldn't cost the earth and wasn't exactly the same as they'd had last week.

He didn't have to do much thinking, really.

It seemed to me that the bar was set so low for men. All I'd have to do in order to be considered a good husband and father would be not to cheat on my wife and not to beat her. If I cooked one meal a week, I'd be a keeper forever. If I stuck my children's clothes in the washing machine and hung them on the line to dry, I'd reach god status.

It would all be so easy for me.

I couldn't blame my mother for not finding another boyfriend after Dad—he'd done so much harm, and anyway, even if she found one of the good ones, it would only mean more work for her. Would it be worth it just to have someone to watch telly with in the evenings? Someone to keep your feet warm in bed?

Mam had the right idea. I was never getting married. If I found someone I liked enough, I'd probably like her too much to make her anyone's wife.

And maybe this had nothing to do with Greta, and maybe it was nothing but nature, but I couldn't understand why men and women tied their minds into tight, complex knots about one another, why it felt so important to humans to be paired up. I'd seen people at school devastated because of a breakup and had seen people—Gwyn and Ela among them—become weakened with pining.

Even my own mother had, at some point, thought that Kelvin would be worth it. And she should have known better, what with all she knew and all that had happened to her.

And Greta had yearned for someone too.

We all knew. Or half knew, because somehow you knew not to ask her questions, not to pry. Once when we were in the park on some Friday night, Ela was drunk and asked her in a cider-stained voice, "So who's this man you're going with? Is it another old one?" And Greta said nothing at all, as if Ela had said nothing. She carried on the conversation she'd been having before and giggled at something, and we all pretended that the question hadn't been asked, although we privately noted the awkwardness, the closed nature of that part of Greta's life.

It was the first I'd heard of any old men, and I was embarrassed to find that the thought hurt me, a short, sharp stab somewhere deep in my stomach. I instantly wanted to know more, much more—*Who's the man? Why don't you want us to know? Do we know him? How old is old? What is it you do together?*

I kept my mouth shut, of course. But after that, I noted the nights out when Greta wasn't present; I noticed when she was with us for an hour and then slung off on her own, wearing more makeup than she normally did, checking her hair all the time with her fingers. I saw her checking her phone sometimes with a faraway look, and I observed the way she sometimes smiled at the screen as if it was a lover and would sometimes put it away, her eyes blank.

"Doesn't your boyfriend mind that we're friends?" I ventured to ask her once, when we were sitting on the mountain, high above the quarry, a rain cloud making its way toward us threateningly. It had taken weeks for me to pluck up the courage to ask the question, and she waved it away as if it was a fly that was attracted to the peach perfume she wore on her throat.

"Don't be stupid," she replied, which didn't answer the question either way. When the rain came, we didn't move. We got wet, and our clothes got heavy, and we watched the cloud pass over us and down the valley.

I knew that she saw someone, or some people, still. Right until the end. On weekends, usually, and late at night.

"I lied for her so many times," Keira told me once after Greta had died. "No one has any idea. There's still a girl code, even though she has died, don't you think, Shaney?"

"Yeah, probably." We were sitting on the benches outside school after the day had ended, eating ice creams that were past their use-by date, which the shop was giving out for free. We'd taken three ice creams each, pretending that the extras were for our friends, and now we each had three cherry-chocolate cones to get through. "Who was he?"

"She never wanted to talk about it. I never even knew if it was the same guy every time or different ones. But she'd tell her parents that she was staying at mine, and then at ten or eleven at night, she'd be off." She bit off a wedge of ice cream and then winced as the cold hit her teeth.

"I wonder whether the cops know."

"Doubt it. She deleted their messages as soon as they came in. Got a new phone quite often too. And I think she messaged through encrypted apps—once she deleted them, there was no trace."

I stuck my tongue into the cone to reach the chocolate. She would have been in so much trouble if her father ever found out. What man was worth that trouble?

Mind you, she'd have been in trouble if her father ever found out that she was friends with me too. And I had no idea why I was worth that risk to her.

"She'd get picked up on the lane behind the quarry," Keira said. "Not far from where she died, actually. God, do you think I should tell the cops?"

"No," I said firmly. "Unless . . . did she ever say that this bloke was unkind to her? Do you think she was abused or something?"

"God, no!" Keira shook her head. "She wouldn't tell me anything about him, but her face lit up whenever she went to meet him or whenever he sent her a message. When I tried to ask her about him, she'd say that she wasn't telling but that I should be happy for her."

"Well, there you go, then. If you tell the cops that she was out late at night with older men—probably married—they'd make her out to be awful. People will say she deserved it."

"Shane!"

"It's true, though. People love thinking that she was a perfect, innocent, virginal type. They don't want to know about real people with real lives."

Keira munched through the second of her ice creams and sat back, her hand on her stomach. "Ela would tell."

"Of course she would. She lives in a safe little world where her mam and dad love her and the police protect her and nothing bad happens to good people. Bless her, but she'd judge Greta herself if she knew about this older man. You know she would."

Keira chewed her lip. She knew that I was talking sense.

"I saw her once, I think." Her voice was quieter now, and monotonous. "It was a Friday night, and I'd gone out for a walk because Mam had her boyfriend over and I felt in the way. Nobody else was out, so I went to the shop to buy a drink and then walked through the park and down that path toward Tregarth."

I nodded, desperate to know more.

"It was only just getting dark. You know that bit at the end of the day when everything's a sort of glowing blue, just before the blackness comes? And when you're out in it, you never realize that it's turned from blue to black until the moment's already gone?"

I knew.

"I was walking home. Had my hood up, my earbuds in. And I didn't hear the car until it passed too close. I jumped."

"It was her?"

"I recognized her hair. It wasn't just blonde, was it, Shaney? It was so shiny and smooth; I never saw hair like it. And the car was a four-by-four, black. I think it was a Mercedes. Looked pretty new, but then what would I know? I think it had something in the front window, like a parking permit? But maybe it was nothing."

I racked my brains for someone I knew who drove a car like that, but there was no one—I don't think I'd ever seen one even driving through the village. "Did you see the guy?"

"It was so quick. I wouldn't be able to pick him out of a lineup or anything. All I noticed was that he had hair that was dark, sort of slick looking, and he was wearing a white shirt. That was all."

"And no number plate?"

Keira looked sideways at me and raised an eyebrow. "This isn't *Crimewatch*, Shane. Of course I didn't get a number plate." She peeled the wrapper off her third ice cream and then looked at me again. "Why would you want the number plate, though? You think this bloke killed her? I should probably tell the cops."

"Nah, I'm just being curious. Look, you can tell the cops if you want to. If it'll make you feel better. It's just, for me . . . anything that will hurt Greta's reputation needs thinking about. It's literally all she has now. I think I'd feel like I was betraying her."

Keira nodded, as I knew she would. If there was anything you could depend on, it was her loyalty to her friends.

It was bad advice, and I knew it even at the time. And I knew that I was on my way to becoming one of the bad men, for manipulating Keira that way.

◆ ◆ ◆

Mr. Lloyd looked like a bullying football coach from a bad American film. He was huge and built squarely, his torso as thick and solid as a wall, and he had one of those strange chunky, veiny necks that people who lift weights sometimes get. When I started school and we had our first assembly, I remember looking at that neck, at the veins bulging out like rivers on a map. They made him look somehow dangerous.

And there were rumors about him, like there were rumors about all the teachers. Apparently, he had a quick temper and was prone to bursts of fury . . . but apparently, the art teacher was living in the storeroom, and apparently, the lab technician was living under an alias after being a key witness in a drug case. None of these things was true, but the rumors gave a ripple of excitement to boring lessons. We didn't want to believe that these people who were in charge of us between nine and three every day were boring, average, normal people with uninteresting lives. Surely people like that couldn't have been handed so much power over us.

I wholeheartedly believed that Mr. Lloyd was the short-tempered brute that people had him down as, though. His size made it easy to imagine, and on the days when Wales was playing rugby and we were allowed to cut classes to watch the match on a huge screen in the hall, I saw the way he yelled at the screen, the muscles in his arms tight and his head and neck a deep, rosy, dangerous red. "*Come on!*" he'd yell, and "*What the hell?*" when the ref made the wrong decision. I wasn't frightened of him, because I kept out of his way, and I'd learned that blending into the background was the best way to avoid the attention of an angry man. But I could see why some of the others were afraid of him.

And then as the years went by, I changed my mind about him. Slowly, almost too slowly for me to notice it myself, I started to almost like him.

He was annoying, of course, but that was part of his job as headmaster. But he made terrible goofy jokes in assembly, and everyone would groan, and he'd grin like an idiot, and that somehow made me like him. He'd come to all the school football and rugby matches, even if it was just year seven, and he'd come into the changing room after everyone was finished and tell them how well they'd done, even if they'd played terribly.

On results day, he'd buy lots of cans and snacks with his own money and set them up in the hall where everyone came to see how they'd done. If they'd done well, he'd say well done and say he was proud; if they'd done badly, he'd find something for them to be proud of, and he'd tell them about it until they felt better. And then he'd talk to them about all the possibilities that lay in front of them, that they could still do anything, exams or no exams. When we'd started our GCSE courses, he gave an assembly to our whole year and droned on for a bit about how it was time for us to knuckle down and start working. He ended it with "Of course you know that exams aren't everything. Don't live your lives thinking that the smartest kids in your year are going to be the most successful in life, because it doesn't happen like that. And remember, there's no moral value to a qualification. You're not a better or worse person just for having passed math. Just do your best." And the teachers all stared at him as if that was the absolute opposite of what they had been teaching us.

Then there was Dion.

It was in year nine, and for a good few weeks, Dion had been gathering darkness and energy like a terrible storm, since his mother had started on the gambling apps again. I knew him well enough to be able to read his silences, and as the threat of his temper got worse and worse, so did my dread. I *knew* he was going to do something awful. I just didn't know what.

Dion wasn't the fighting type—he was cleverer than that. So it turned out that when he did boil over that time, I wasn't even there.

It was awful.

You don't need to know about it.

It's enough to tell you that social services had to get involved with his family again, that they had to develop an action plan for him, and that he had to have counseling (where he sat in silence the entire time, an hour a week for six weeks). And we were all sure that he'd finally be expelled.

But what Mr. Lloyd did was invite Dion to his office—only Dion, not his mam, because she wasn't the type to respond well to authority and her presence would make Dion defensive. Dion almost didn't go. Didn't see the point. But his curiosity, and his boredom after a week's suspension, got the better of him. Plus, he'd heard so much about Mr. Lloyd's famous temper. He wanted to see how angry the headmaster could get. He almost wanted to be punched in the face, to be the one who finally made Mr. Lloyd snap.

But Dion had underestimated him.

He'd been shown into Mr. Lloyd's office by a receptionist that couldn't look Dion in the eye, but Mr. Lloyd looked up from his computer with a smile, invited Dion to sit down, shut the door behind him. He'd fetched himself a can of Coke and had taken a long glug before apologizing. "Sorry, d'you want one? I keep cases of them underneath my desk. No sugar-free, though, I'm afraid." And Dion shook his head, too suspicious to accept.

"How you doing, then?" Mr. Lloyd asked lightly. "Do you prefer being off school?"

Dion shrugged his shoulders, giving nothing away.

"I'm just wondering whether I should exclude you permanently or not. The governing body wants me to but has left it up to me, ultimately." He took another glug of Coke. "I was just wondering what would make you happiest."

To Dion, this felt like a trap. Teachers could be tricksy like that. Some of them liked a project, taking on the troubled kid as if they were in some crappy nineties Hollywood film, where either algebra, Shakespeare, or quantum physics could save a doomed kid from his own fate. Dion wasn't going to let any teacher be the savior of him. He said nothing.

"They could send you to a special school, but I don't reckon you'll go there much. And I've been looking at your results here. Predicted grades aren't bad at all. You've got mates here. It's just, I don't want you to carry on coming here if you don't like it. If it makes you so miserable that you do things that land you in hot water. You can't keep on hurting people, Dion."

It wasn't a telling off. Mr. Lloyd was simply setting out the options in front of Dion. He didn't sound angry or even disappointed—his voice was level and calm. And he wasn't the type of man who could fake calmness. "If you want to know my opinion, I reckon if you get expelled now, you'll end up in jail. I'm not judging. But you could stay on, keep your head down, and actually get a job and a good life."

And Dion hated the fact that Mr. Lloyd was right, but he knew that he was, and he also knew that he could tell the head teacher to piss off and walk away from this school and its stupid rules and boring classes forever or he could swallow his pride and make a better decision for once.

Dion later told me that if Mr. Lloyd had been different, he would have walked away. If he'd been told off yet again or if the head teacher had tried to make out that he was doing him a favor or that he was angry or disappointed or any of the other layers of manipulation adults wrap around young people, he would have gone. But he didn't. Dion knew he could make the right decision without feeling like he'd lost an argument.

"I'll stay, then," he said, his voice tight as a fist.

"Nice one," said Mr. Lloyd. "And come here to me if you feel like you're losing it, okay?"

Dion nodded—though, he wasn't sure that he would.

And when it was time for him to leave, Dion just stood there, not going, just staring at the wall awkwardly because, for some reason, he needed to know the truth about Mr. Lloyd. He needed to know if he could *really* trust him or if this was all a clever ruse.

"Is there something else, Dion?"

"There's a rumor that the painting of the quarry is there to cover up a hole in the wall where you punched it."

Mr. Lloyd raised his eyebrows and grinned. "Bloody hell, really?" he said brightly. "Why do they think I punched a wall?"

"I dunno," said Dion, suddenly feeling a bit silly.

"Take a look if you want." And Dion did. Of course there was no hole in the wall—he even ran his hand over it to see if the plaster was different. It wasn't. "The painting was a present from the headmaster before me. I don't like it, really; it's a gloomy old thing to be staring at all day. I'd rather have a photo of the Wales rugby squad, but I don't think people would like that."

Dion hung the picture back on the wall and took a step back.

There were holes all over the walls of his home.

"See you next week, then, Dion," said Mr. Lloyd cheerfully, and he never mentioned it ever again, never gave Dion funny, knowing looks in the corridors, never singled him out.

But I don't think I realized how much I liked Mr. Lloyd until Greta died, and everything became strange, and he suddenly found himself the head of a school in mourning. All eyes were on him to tell us what to do, how to be. And how was he supposed to know? He was only a PE teacher who had somehow found himself further up the career ladder than he'd ever expected to be.

It was months and months later that Ela told us about him, maybe even a year after Greta died. It was secondhand information, of course, because Ela's mother was a school friend of Mr. Lloyd's wife, and they occasionally got together for boozy bottomless brunches with their other friends and updated their life stories. And I knew that Ela had a tendency to enhance the truth in order to ensure a good story and that I could never fully trust her version of how things had been for Mr. Lloyd at that time. But then I did exactly the same, and the more I recalled the things she had said, the more I added to them, until, by the end, the story of Mr. Lloyd played out in my mind like a movie based on a true story. I trusted my instincts enough to feel that it was probably true. He was a good guy.

Greta's death had nearly broken Mr. Lloyd.

He would never ever say it out loud, not even to his own friends—for a long time, not even to Sharon, his wife, even when he desperately wanted to. He didn't want to make it all about him. But from that first Sunday when he was told what had happened to one of his pupils, a sense of horror filled him and stayed with him.

It was just so much responsibility.

He'd liked Greta in that benign, distant way that teachers liked pupils—she was an easy pupil, never had detention, never gave him any cause to worry. There were others that favored her for being smart and pretty and cool, but not Mr. Lloyd. He didn't really have favorites, and he never seemed to hate any of the kids either, even the ones that were easy to hate.

When he heard, he was in his garage, tinkering about in the engine of Sharon's car, which had started to rattle. The police pulled up, and he knew something awful had happened, probably to his elderly mother, perhaps to one of Sharon's brothers. He and Sharon didn't have children. They'd wanted to, with a silent, aching desperation, thumbing tiny onesies longingly in shops and swallowing back an uneasy sorrow whenever anyone else announced a pregnancy. They'd had all the tests. Something was wrong with Sharon's eggs, and they were told that they would never have a baby, and after a few days of digesting this news, Sharon sat him down and asked for a divorce. She loved him, but she wanted him to be a father and couldn't bear to take that possibility away from him. Mr. Lloyd just stood up and enveloped her in his arms—she was a short, round woman with impossibly frizzy blonde hair and huge hazel eyes—and he didn't speak for a long time. And then he just said that he loved her, and that was that. The longing for a baby didn't go away, but they were happy.

For some reason, the absence of their baby came into Mr. Lloyd's mind just as those cops slammed the doors of their cars and put their hats on their heads. He wondered if they *had* had a baby, how old would it be now? Boy or girl? What would it look like?

He spent the next few weeks in a state of constant worry, his stomach churning, always waiting for something else that would need his attention or care. He'd had to go to Bryn Mawr to share his condolences, of course, and that was difficult enough. Was it normal that no one seemed to be crying? Was it odd that Liz was chatting with him as if the loss of her daughter was just another story and had moved the conversation on to the traffic in the village on three-day weekends and the price of bus fares these days?

It must be the shock, Mr. Lloyd thought, swallowing back the impression he'd always had that the Pugh family were just a bit strange, a bit cagey.

Then there had been the police presence in the school, which made him feel sick and out of control and as if the safe, happy feeling he'd tried to create in his school was damaged by the constant interruption of strangers.

He wasn't keen on Call Me Karen.

He and Sharon spoke in the evenings over dinners that he would barely pick at. Sharon, in turn, would create more and more complex dishes, grand feasts to try and tempt him to eat more, and then when he wouldn't, she'd be up, unable to sleep, worrying about her husband and grieving for a girl she didn't know, and she'd eat all his leftovers herself. Mr. Lloyd starved his grief, but his wife fed hers.

"What's she like?" Sharon asked about Call Me Karen, and Mr. Lloyd shrugged. He had tried to share as little as possible with Sharon, not wanting to burden her, not seeing that she was desperate for him to talk to her, for him not to shut her out of his misery. Mr. Lloyd stared down at his plate, looking huge and strong and yet so weak sitting there, unable to eat even a salad.

"She's trying her best to come across as warm," he replied, which was a kind way of saying *She's faking kindness.* "The kids aren't falling for it. They're either terrified of her or they think she's pathetic."

Sharon nodded, her brow furrowed. "Has she been talking to you?"

"All the time. *All the time.*" And it was one of the most difficult things, unexpectedly, because Mr. Lloyd wanted to be with the kids, in the classes, spending time with them, seeing how they were doing. But every time he had a spare five minutes, it was "Can I have a word?" and "Is there anything you can remember that might be significant?"

He was the last to leave the school each night. For some reason, he checked the whole place as if he was checking his own home before going to bed. Were the doors locked? Windows fastened tight? Nobody left behind? Nobody forgotten?

They were the times he allowed himself to cry.

After breaking down in that first assembly after Greta's death, Mr. Lloyd had kept all his tears and emotions tied up tight inside of him like a well-kept secret. He never again cried in assemblies, didn't even cry as he gave the eulogy at the funeral. Didn't cry with his wife as she wrapped her arms around him in bed at night, stroking his hair like a child.

But in those silent, still corridors in the early evenings, when the colors of sunsets would bleed over the jagged edges of the quarry and through the school windows, glazing the old school photos on the walls, the rubber-sole stains on the floors, the abandoned lockers and coat hooks, he cried. It seemed to him that this horrible tragedy had broken everything. That this place was nothing but a place of grief now. And more than that, he wept fat, ugly tears for Greta, who should have been just another face in the crowd, moaning about homework and a forgotten math book.

To Mr. Lloyd, for the rest of his life, nothing, but nothing, would come close to the sadness of a school that had lost a pupil. There was no tragedy like it.

Weeks and weeks after Greta died, Call Me Karen was in again, looking for clues that weren't there, picking random groups of kids out of classes and questioning them for no discernible reason.

"Can you tell me why you chose to talk to that particular group?" Mr. Lloyd asked her one day after she'd been quizzing a group of year sevens. "They were years younger than Greta; I doubt there's any connection."

He was polite enough, but Call Me Karen was spiky, constantly irritated by the lack of leads. "I can't divulge that information."

Because there's nothing to divulge, Mr. Lloyd thought. *You're just randomly picking kids out of classes for this.* "It's just that it can be distressing for them, being taken out of classes and questioned like this. We've had a few tears. Some parents have been asking why their kids seem to be interviewed when they'd never said a word to Greta."

"There's a support officer in every chat—chat, not interview—to look after the needs of the children. And of course there's the counselor."

"I understand you're interviewing the teachers again too. You've pulled in a Welsh teacher three times, and she has never taught Greta, and they had no connection."

Call Me Karen looked up at Mr. Lloyd then, squared her shoulders, and took a long, deep breath. "I'm trying to catch a killer, Mr. Lloyd. Do you have any objection to that?"

"And I'm trying to look after a whole fucking town that's broken by grief." Mr. Lloyd said it quietly, looking at the floor, and regretted the swearing as soon as he had said it. He didn't trust Call Me Karen with something as important as the job she'd been given.

"Let us both do our jobs, then," she said, her tone clipped, and she left to go and find some other random children to worry. She would never understand this town and how precious it was, would never understand the understated and unspoken care shared between its people. She just wanted to solve the mystery, lock someone up, feel good about herself. She didn't understand that this whole valley needed the same care and attention as was given to Greta's memory. She didn't see that every single person in this school, in this village was just as important as Greta.

He realized that Call Me Karen had no hope at all of solving this crime. She didn't understand the world in which it had been committed.

He was a good man, Mr. Lloyd—naturally a good man, instinctively a decent person. He was normal and flawed and imperfect, of course, but above all, he was careful of others. And that's why I decided that I'd been wrong about men and that maybe I didn't have to be like the others I knew. There were lots like Mr. Lloyd too. Normal, careful, quietly kind men, who never punched walls, who held their wives' hands as they watched telly, and who loved entire villages, even the bad kids, without ever saying much about it at all.

CHAPTER 10

I started obsessing about Kelvin Pugh.

For a while, I was thinking about him more than I thought about Greta. In all the quiet times, in all the empty spaces in my day, my mind would make its way back to that house and to him and Mam sharing coffee and secrets and looks over the kitchen table. I couldn't help myself. I'd imagine what his face would look like when he was flirting with her, the exact twist of his mouth as he smiled. And I'd think about Mam, too, about that period of time when she'd fancied him. What kind of looks did she give him? Did she make herself prettier for work, wear a bit of makeup, do her hair, wear a spritz of the cheap perfume I'd bought her for Christmas?

It's so, so easy to become consumed by thoughts that turn your stomach.

In a math lesson or sharing a smoke with Dion and Gwyn on the way home from school or waiting in line to buy a drink at Tesco. They'd flash into my mind, until I was sure of just one thing.

I hated Kelvin Pugh.

It was early one evening on a filthy, wet night a few weeks after Greta's death, when being out alone at night still felt disjointed and weird, when I wandered down to the little shop on the corner to get myself a chocolate bar. Mam had fallen asleep in front of the telly again, and I couldn't settle myself to do anything. Homework was too boring, gaming online with the boys was too still. I needed to get out. I sneaked out knowing that Mam wouldn't wake, wouldn't miss me.

I didn't notice that it was Mary in front of me in the queue until I smelled her. She was odd in that way—her scent was unexpectedly old fashioned, not unpleasant but as if she was wearing her grandmother's perfume, rose or violet or lily of the valley. I hadn't even noticed it properly before, but I realized then, in that queue, that it made Mary different. Her whole presence was unlike the other girls in our school.

I looked at her, at the way she stood, slightly stooped over, her neck somehow long and craning. She was wearing an old raincoat that was too big for her and jogging trousers with battered, old trainers. Her thin, lanky hair, the color of mud, hung around her shoulders. I couldn't see her face, but I knew it well enough—pale, gray eyed, thin lipped. Plain. She was one of the invisible ones, too, but there was a weight that seemed to hang around her shoulders like it tended to do on older women, women who had been burdened with too much work and responsibility and life. Women like my mam.

I watched as she passed the bag of plain crisps over to the cashier and paid her money. I heard her breathy, monotone *thanks*. She didn't realize that it was me behind her until she turned to leave, but she didn't say anything to me even then. We weren't friends. We weren't anything to one another. I don't think we'd ever spoken.

"All right, Mary?" I said, surprising myself. I don't know why I greeted her. I don't know why I was kind, why my voice was so gentle when I said her name. But it seemed to be all connected—Greta and Kelvin and what had happened to Mary.

"All right," she replied, her eyes widening in surprise that I had said a word to her. And then she ducked down her craning neck again, placed her hood over her head, and went out into the filthy night, leaving nothing but the scent of another time behind her.

◆　◆　◆

It had been a teacher.

Or a tutor, as he called himself, because it didn't happen at school, and he wasn't qualified. Her mother had signed her up for art classes when she was in year seven, because they were cheap, and it was a small group that met in the village hall every Thursday evening. And because, although she'd never admit this, Mary's mother had wanted more than anything for her daughter to be someone special, someone creative, and as the years went by, Mary hadn't shown any signs of being either of those things. But she was good at copying anime characters into her sketchbook, so art it was.

The tutor was called Thom, and he was teaching art because he wasn't earning enough money making it himself. He had shown promise when he was young, and he'd become briefly famous in the area for painting landscapes in bold acrylic colors, but then his work had fallen out of favor and out of fashion. Now he did some design work for private companies, a few logos for local cafés or shops, and he taught evening classes for children who were either well on their way to being more talented than him or weren't all that talented in the first place.

None of our gang went to the art classes, of course, although Keira might have gone if she had felt that it was cool enough—she was good at art. No one took much notice of the classes—most people went to something, either art or dance or drama or hockey. I never went to anything, and neither did Dion. School was more than enough for us, and who had the spare money to spend on a hobby?

We only found out later what Thom was really like.

I'd seen him around—he was the type of man who wanted to be seen and noticed, and he tried his best to look arty. He wore patterned silk shirts, loose trousers, and bold-colored shoes that looked expensive. His black hair was slicked almost greasily over his shirt collar but was receding at the front, and his face was almost good looking in a severe way, his dark eyes hooded and his thin lips wide and pink. He didn't live in Bethesda but a few towns over—far enough that we wouldn't really know him or his wife or his grown-up children.

When Mary started going to his classes, her life was transformed.

He told her she was wonderful. So, so talented! He told her that she should be thinking about art school and painting and maybe illustrating books or writing graphic novels. He'd grin at her when she came in. When he saw her mother at the end of those first batch of lessons, he'd call her "my star pupil." He would recommend artists she should look out for, and she'd go home and look them up, wanting to feed back to him some information at the next lesson so she could prove that she was listening to him.

Mary bloomed like a spring dandelion when she started to go to those lessons, became less shy, started laughing out loud at jokes at school instead of swallowing back any sounds. She was going to be an artist. She was going to have a life, not just a series of dull, predictable decades.

She held on to that hope. For a while, anyway. As long as he allowed her to.

He was an angry man.

There are lots and lots of angry men—God knows I know that better than anyone. But Thom was not violent or loud in his anger, and so he could pretend to himself that he was a good guy. Sometimes, his classes—only four or five pupils, usually shy or unconfident ones—were terrified of him. He was cruel in his temper, dismissive of pupils' work, and careless with their feelings. He sneered at their paintings, rolled his eyes at someone's experiments with watercolor or linocut. He'd call their work horrible names that were too long and complicated to understand.

And yet sometimes, he was wonderful.

Sometimes, he'd be in a kind mood and would fizz around the room, complimenting everyone, calling them all artists. He'd make tiny recommendations that would lift a dull painting into an interesting one, or he would teach a pupil a slightly different angle to hold a pencil that would transform their work. Those days would be magical. Everyone would feel like friends, like artists, and the chat between the group and their teacher made them feel like they were all clever enough, good enough. When he was good, he was so very good that it was almost addictive. Everyone longed for his attention, his compliments. Even the ones, like Mary, who weren't all that interested in art to begin with suddenly wanted to become artists—even if only to please Thom.

And then slowly and after a few months, he seemed to take a dislike to Mary.

After the truth came out, people tried to coax the other pupils in the group to tell the story, but it didn't happen that way. Thom had drilled into them some strange, sick loyalty so that although they knew what had happened and had seen what he was like, their tongues felt bound. They only told their very closest friends in whispers, and then they told their friends, and slowly the extent of his cruelty became known.

Thom bullied Mary.

It's such a small word, with so much power. A grown man in his forties suddenly decided to deride all the artwork created by this small, mousy, shy fourteen-year-old, would laugh at her attempts to begin with and then become angry. Her failure to draw an accurate portrait infuriated him; the lack of movement in the trees she painted gave him the rage. He seemed to think that she wasn't trying hard enough, although she was trying harder and harder each week, desperate for the praise that he'd once showered her with.

He pushed her easel over when she mixed her green paints too vividly, and snarled when she shrank away, afraid.

He tore up the pencil drawing she'd made of her cousin's baby—the best drawing she'd ever done, something she'd pored over for hours at home until her eyes stung with the concentration. She had brought it in proudly, planning to frame it and give it as a gift. Thom then placed the two halves of the paper on the desk in front of her so that she could see the torn-up baby. "You can do better!" he said, his voice dangerously quiet.

When she drew her beloved anime characters, Thom held them up in front of the rest and explained how "Mary will never be an artist.

Can you see why? No originality. No technique. There's just nothing to see here." And when she had cried, having tried her best to swallow down the tears before they spilled out of her, Thom looked puzzled. "So sensitive! It's very important that you all learn not to take things personally. The art world can be very cruel." And the rest nodded and agreed because it was clear that Thom expected them to, but each and every one of them knew that Mary was crying because Thom had given her hope of a happy future, and then he'd taken it away.

They all knew that it felt wrong. That it felt like someone should step in. But they were teenagers, and he was an adult, so it must have been acceptable after all—maybe this was how things were in the adult world.

I don't know what else Thom did to her. There were some stories that were obviously made up by people who loved the drama, and others that I could almost believe. I don't believe he ever touched her, not ever—not to push, hit, or shove her, nor for any other reason either. I don't believe he ever sent her an inappropriate message or visited her home or did anything like that. He just seemed to enjoy tormenting her in class. Lavishing her with praise and attention and then watching how his words had a devastating effect on her, extinguishing any light that had appeared in her eyes. And he enjoyed watching how the others did nothing, too, although they were meant to be her friends. It was so much easier for them to stand by and be silent.

You don't have to touch a person in order to harm them. You don't have to break any laws in order to break a person. Some people make it into an art.

One art lesson was particularly bad. Thom had praised the work of all the others and had spent time explaining the strengths of each piece: "Gareth, your shading is exquisite here," and "Your piece is so atmospheric, Amelie; it has so much beautiful gloom." When it came to Mary's painting—an odd, vivid, actually quite clever picture of a bowl of fruit but with the colors deliberately inverted—Thom simply said,

"No." He sighed, caught Mary's eye, and then moved on to the next person.

It was just too much for her.

The next day at school, she didn't get up from her seat at the end of registration like the others did, didn't move to get ready for the first class. She just sat there. The teacher tried talking to her. "Mary? Are you okay?" But Mary said nothing. The teacher moved over to her and noticed that she was picking at the skin around her fingers and that they were bleeding. "Can I take you to see Mr. Lloyd?" the teacher asked gently, and Mary gave a light nod and walked with her to the headmaster's office.

I don't know what was said in there, but Mary was sent home for the rest of the day and the next week, just to rest and to catch up on sleep. The following Thursday evening, Mary didn't go to the art class, but someone else did—Mr. Lloyd, who instructed all the pupils to stay outside for a while because he needed to chat with Thom. There was no yelling, but when Mr. Lloyd left the hall ten minutes later, it was with a certain energy, and Thom was twitchy and tetchy throughout the lesson.

Mr. Lloyd hung Mary's painting of the bowl of fruit outside his office, where every visitor to the school could see it. He and the school's art teacher tried to get Mary to join the school art club when she came back, but her heart wasn't in it. She was good—Thom had, ironically, been a good teacher—but she hated the way it made her feel now. Just the smell of paint was enough to make her feel uncomfortable.

It was one of the first things that Greta and I disagreed about. Mary. We'd been going on one of our walks through the dense woodland on the hill behind the village, although it was private, and we were trespassing. There was no footpath, so we clambered over dead branches and felt them snapping like dry bones beneath our feet, and we tripped a hundred times over vines or brambles. It was always twilight in those woods, and I didn't like it, but of course I always followed Greta in there. "It's private," she'd say as though that was the most important thing.

She didn't want to be seen with me.

"I want to say something to her," she said once we'd found an old fallen tree to sit on to smoke and eat sweets. "Poor Mary."

"It's not *that* big of a deal," I replied. "Thom is an arsehole; there are lots of those about. Not much you can do about it."

Wisps of Greta's hair had stuck to her lips—she pulled them away, tucked them behind her ear. She was wearing a huge gray hoody over jeans and her battered, muddy walking boots. She hadn't made an effort, which on the one hand frustrated me—I wasn't important enough to dress up for—but on the other hand pleased me. She was comfortable enough in my company not to feel the need to bother with wearing anything fussy or to do her makeup.

"It's a *massive* big deal," she scolded me, looking genuinely hurt that I hadn't realized this. "This might ruin Mary's life. He took away her hope. He should be in jail."

"Okay, and for what crime?" I asked—though, I had no sympathy with Thom at all. Sometimes it was fun to disagree just for the sake of it. "For tearing up a pencil drawing? For saying unkind things about her work? I'm not saying it's okay to be like him, but it's not against the law."

"Then the law isn't good enough."

I reached into the pink-and-white-striped sweet bag on my lap and explored what was left from the pick'n'mix I'd paid a fortune for. White chocolate mousse. Ace. Greta took one last drag from her cigarette and threw it onto the ground where there was nothing but a thick, crisp, dry layer of fallen pine needles. I jumped on it to stamp it out.

"Bloody hell, Greta, you could have set the whole place on fire. You're a disaster area."

"Isn't it weird that people go to jail for not paying bills, but a bloke like that Thom can bully a young girl, and there's literally no punishment? He's still running the art class!"

"And the parents are still sending in their kids. They know what he's been accused of, but they still send them in."

"They want their kids to be good artists more than they want to keep them safe."

I looked over at Greta, who was trying to light yet another cigarette with a lighter that was almost out of fuel. She seemed agitated that day, her movement jerky and unlike her. I don't know why, but what happened to Mary disturbed her.

"You should make friends with her."

"Mary?" Greta looked up at me. She had a tiny, tiny smear of yesterday's mascara under her left eye—it looked like a black, broken vein. She thought about what I'd said for a minute and then shook her head. "Nah."

"Why not? She'd love being friends with you. She could be in your gang."

"I don't have a gang!"

I grinned. "Of course you do! You and Ela and Keira. The popular girls!"

Greta shook her head, pursing her lips in annoyance slightly snobbishly. "Popular! Give it a rest."

"You *know* it's true."

The lighter finally flickered to life—she lit her cigarette and took a long drag. "I couldn't suddenly be her friend, though, could I? Because it would look as if I only wanted to be her mate because she'd been abused."

I took another sweet from the bag. Fizzy cola bottle. Yum. "Well, I never heard you even say her name before all this came out."

Greta let out the smoke, dragon-like, through her nostrils. That seemed to make her think. I was half expecting her to berate me for it, but she said nothing.

"Or you could be her friend in secret. So that only you two know about it. Meet her on the mountain or in fields or, I dunno, in the woodlands."

And I turned my back because, for a moment, I allowed myself to feel the hurt that I was a secret friend, someone to be hidden away.

◆ ◆ ◆

We barely spoke about Mary after that. Things moved on, and there were other, more recent, tragedies to discuss.

Life carried on.

Just once, a few weeks after Greta and I had talked about Mary, I saw them together. Well, not really together, but there was an unexpected togetherness, too, a little thing that jumped out at me.

I was in school, between lessons, and walking behind Greta and Keira to our history class. I was looking in my bag as I walked, because I had a cereal bar in there somewhere and I was having one of those days where I was constantly starving hungry. My fingers found it under my schoolbooks, and as I pulled it out, I raised my eyes.

Mary was passing Greta in the opposite direction, on her way to some other class, and I happened to catch a second between them—a tiny smile, almost shy, eyes locked. And then they looked away and carried on, and I knew that Greta had said something to Mary, that a secret connection had been made, although I would never know anything more than that.

I wondered how many of us secret friends she had, and whether she only collected damaged people.

CHAPTER 11

So. DCI Karen Davies.

She was the boss. That much was clear. The other coppers were just doing what she told them to, and they'd follow her around the place as if she was Jesus. I'd noticed, of course, when she came over to question Mam that she was playing a game. Good cop, bad cop—I'd only seen that kind of thing in TV programs before now. I didn't think they actually did it in real life. In my experience, every cop was a bad cop, and that was still probably true; they just became more sly and manipulative when they were investigating something big like a murder. They were making people feel safe by pretending to be just like the rest of us.

She seemed so nice, and people like that are always the ones you should watch out for.

Break time on the Monday after the funeral, Dion and I went over to the all-weather sports fields—he wanted a smoke, he said, and the rest of the gang wouldn't come because it was spitting rain. Gwyn and Ela were snogging somewhere—he'd obviously taken my advice about her—and I think that Keira was pissed off with us all after Thursday night when Ela revealed that Gwyn and Greta had been together the night she died. She stayed in the art classroom with a sheet of paper the size of a dining table, and pots containing deep pools of red and purple and black. Dion asked if she wanted to come, and she snarled, "Just piss off, okay?" So we left her alone, knowing that she was sinking into one of her silent days.

"I'm glad they didn't come," said Dion, cupping his cigarette to shield it from the wind as he lit it. "I've been sniffing around."

"Oh?"

"I don't like all this about Gwyn and Greta. Someone's gonna crack. Someone's gonna tell that copper."

"You reckon?"

"Defo."

I sighed and shook my head when he offered me a toke on his smoke. I didn't fancy it. "They came over the other day. That DCI Karen and that fat copper with the wanky hair."

"What? To your house?"

"Yeah. Nothing to do with me. Mam's their cleaner, isn't she. Well, she was. I dunno if she still is."

"Oh!" Dion nodded, relieved that they hadn't come over to question me.

"He'd been perving on her. Kelvin. Greta's dad. Trying it on with Mam." My voice was flat and quiet, but Dion knew me well. He'd have been able to hear the rage in the way I was holding it all in. He didn't look shocked; he just shook his head and blew out a lungful of smoke.

"People with money think that every single fucking thing is for sale."

He was a quiet lad, but Dion knew how things were, and he knew how to say the words I needed.

"Thanks, Dion."

"Don't be a nob."

I smiled and looked down.

"I've been doing my homework about this Karen."

"What for?" I asked, surprised.

"Dunno. I don't like that she knows everything about us and we don't know anything about her."

"But she *doesn't* know everything about us. She hardly knows anything at all."

"Well, anyway, you never know when this kind of thing might come in useful."

Jesus Christ. He must have thought he was in a crappy mafia film from 1975. "And?"

"She comes from Carmarthenshire. Young-farmers type. She was mad about ponies when she was younger, you know the sort. She lives in Wrexham with her husband, Nigel. They do marathons, and they've got a camper van they travel about in at the weekends to do outdoorsy stuff. Two kids, Oliver and Hetty. They're five, and they go to the Welsh school, but they speak English at home."

"How the hell d'you know all this?"

"Doesn't matter, does it? She doesn't use her real name on Facebook, because she's a copper. She's called Karen Jamiroquai on there, after some shit band from the nineties."

"I really don't get why we need to know all this."

"She goes home sometimes after being here but mostly stays in the Travelodge because it gets so late. She'd prefer a place to stay here in Bethesda, but there aren't any hotels, are there, and she doesn't want to stay in a holiday home."

"Do you do any homework at all?"

"This bit's important. She thinks that there's something people aren't telling her about Greta. Something big. She reckons it might be to do with her family but that we—our gang, I mean—know more than we're letting on."

"Well she's not that bad of a detective, then, is she." I smiled the kind of smile that has nothing to do with joy. "How the hell do you know what she's thinking?"

"She's asking people questions about us. Whether we do drugs, whether we sleep together. She's like a dog with a bone, Shane. Greta's death is on the front page of every newspaper, on every channel. It's not going away. They want someone locked up for this."

I shook my head. "You think I don't already know this?"

Dion flicked his smoke on the floor. "You don't seem bothered!"

"They're watching us, you idiot. Whatever we do, they're watching. If they see us getting worked up, we have no hope. Act normal, okay? Pretend that none of this is happening. As long as we all keep our mouths shut, we're okay."

"Yeah. Yeah, that makes sense." Dion nodded, and for once, I could see the smallest hint of panic in him, in the way he pressed his lips tight. I hadn't realized how worried he was. "But look, we've got to get rid of the . . ."

Dion was the biggest psycho I knew. And I knew a lot of nutters. I'd known him when he was just a little boy, and I remembered the way he used to coax cats into his uncle's shed in order to hurt them, just to know what it felt like to harm a living thing. And I don't know exactly what happened between him and some thin, quiet kid called Jacob when we were in year seven; I only knew that the two of them had gone to the quarry after school one day to smoke cigarettes and that Jacob had arrived home just after nine that night, shaking with fear, his trousers sopping wet where he'd pissed himself. He never accused Dion of anything, but he never came back to school, and apparently he had some kind of breakdown a few months later.

But I wasn't afraid of Dion—he'd never hurt me, we had too much history—but if I was honest with myself, which I rarely was, I thought that other people should be afraid of him. The most frightening thing about him was that he was so good at hiding the fact that he was a psycho.

He didn't look tough now; he didn't seem dangerous. I was in control—he was nothing but a kid terrified that the world was finally going to catch him out.

"I'm sorting it." My voice was steady, and I felt fine. No nerves.

"Yeah, but what are you gonna do? If you get caught . . ."

"For fuck's sake, Dion. I'm not gonna get caught."

"How will you get rid of them?"

"I'm not gonna tell you. That's for the best. Stop thinking about it. It's gone. It never happened."

"Okay. Thanks, Shane." At the far end of the field, the school bell rang like a shrill call to arms, and we started walking back toward our next lesson, the rain a soft mist around us.

◆　◆　◆

The Welsh department in our school is down a long corridor, then has a few steps going up. Three classrooms and one storeroom.

Miss Jenkins's room is on the left. She's one of the nicest teachers at school, and probably one of the best too. She's kind to everyone, doesn't lose her temper, but doesn't take any nonsense either. I didn't hate my lessons with her, although I could never be bothered with books or any of that, and poetry's just a waste of words. But at least she tried to make things interesting.

There was a big storeroom leading off the classroom. It was full of the kinds of junk you'd expect—piles of books, papers that are curling at the edges, a shelf of videotapes but no VCR to play them. This was where Miss Jenkins kept her coat and bag, too, hanging on a hook on the back of the door. The room smelled like dust and paper and a little bit like Miss Jenkins's perfume.

There was a photo in a frame on the storeroom wall, a huge, heavy frame that almost filled the wall. It was an old photo of a man with thick glasses, his hair slicked back, wet looking, and he wasn't smiling, but he didn't look angry or sad either. It was one of those photos that seemed to stare right at you wherever you were standing. He was some author from Bethesda, a famous man if you happened to be into reading books, which I wasn't. Miss Jenkins adored him. That's why this photo was hanging in her storeroom, like some weird shrine, like a teenage girl would have for her favorite pop star on her bedroom wall.

Later that day, I left the canteen after lunch and told the boys I'd be out to play footie in a while. I walked up the corridor to the Welsh department and straight into Miss Jenkins's room. There were three sixth-form girls in there, chatting over their lunchboxes. They stopped talking and looked up at me when I walked in.

The key to being a good liar is to believe a little bit in the lie.

"Gotta get a book," I said sullenly, and the girls turned away. I was of no interest to them.

I slid into the storeroom.

Under the framed photo of Caradog Pritchard—that was the name of the author—there was a long, low shelf laden with old, faded copies of novels that people had long forgotten about. They were dusty, but not as dusty as they had been.

I'd moved them a couple of weeks ago.

I pulled out a few handfuls of books and put my hand into the empty space behind. Yes, it was all still there. I removed the items and stuffed them into my school backpack. I put the books back on the shelf, exactly as they had been, and then changed my mind and grabbed one. After all, I'd told those sixth-form girls that I was here to get a book—it would look odd if I left without one.

I glimpsed at the title of the book, *Un Nos Ola Leuad—One Moonlit Night*. It had been written by Caradog Pritchard, the bloke in the photo. I looked up at him, and he stared back, as if he could see all the way across the years, right at what I was doing. *Thanks for the alibi,* I thought, before leaving the storeroom and the classroom and the Welsh department and the school with Greta's phone and bag hidden in my backpack and a book I would never read in my hand.

CHAPTER 12

Sleeping bag. Clothes (not too many). Cash, and lots of it. Cheap smartphone, bought from a supermarket for fifty quid, and throwaway, untraceable SIM cards to go with it. Cereal bars, just for the first part of the plan, and other nonperishable foods that needed no cooking, like crappy pastries that had frighteningly long use-by dates, crisps, nuts, and noodles.

"Noodles?" I asked. "But you can't cook."

"Ramen noodles are lovely uncooked," Greta said. I raised an eyebrow at her, and she tore open a packet, offered me a thin sheet of hard noodles. I crunched into it.

"God. It *is* nice."

"Told you."

She had found us a space. It belonged to her father, like most things seemed to around here, but the barn at the foot of the mountain, under the shadow of the quarry, and always threatening to be flooded by the nearby stream—well, it was worthless to Kelvin and too far from the farm to bother with anyway. He'd never really used it, and it was far enough from the village that it wasn't being used by kids to smoke and get off.

We stood in the middle, looking at all the stuff Greta had brought with her.

"You could stay here for a while, you know. I'll bring you food. And whatever else you need."

She shook her head, her ponytail bouncing in the half light of the barn. "Thanks, Shaney, but I'm better off leaving before they realize I'm gone. I'll be impossible to find in a city."

Greta never looked as well as she did when she started believing she could run away.

I hadn't tried to give her the idea, but it had inadvertently come from me. We'd been walking along the wall that led to the woods, and she'd been telling me about how her father had decided that every night, he would be checking her phone for unsuitable messages, apps, or internet use.

"God. My mother would have a heart attack if she saw half the things I've seen online," I guffawed, before instantly regretting it in case it made Greta think I was a weird pervert. But she just nodded vigorously.

"Exactly! I mean, I learn more on there than I've ever done at school—not good stuff, all of it, but we need to know as much as possible, right?"

"Mm-hmm."

"And now, I have to delete all my messages as soon as they come in, and I've deleted some of my apps because I don't want him to see . . . not that there's much to see anyway, but I still don't want my dad on there!"

"I get it."

"Honest to God, they're *nuts*, Shaney. I wish they were more like your mam. I wish they paid her for parenting lessons instead of paying her to clean."

"I wish they paid her for both," I said, half joking. "You *could* just run away."

"Not really, because I . . ." And she stopped, and I saw the thought sink in. "I could, really, couldn't I?"

"Yeah. You're not a child. You could get away somewhere, get a job. Start again."

She seemed to stand taller then, pulling back her shoulders and lifting her chin a bit. I don't know if anyone else in the world had noticed it, but she had a habit of licking her lips whenever she was excited or when something interested her. It was a childlike gesture, innocent and sweet, and always made me want to smile, although I suppressed it because it would make me seem soppy.

"They'd come after me," she said gently, softly, and I knew she wanted me to disagree with her.

"They'd try, but then don't leave a trail."

"Do you really think I could?"

"Anyone can walk away from anywhere. You just have to decide to do it."

She grinned at me, a true, wide, toothy grin where she wasn't trying to look beautiful or coy or sexy or cool, just *her*, just a real, authentic Greta smile.

They were so rare for someone who smiled so much.

A few days later, I was summoned for another walk, and that's when Greta grabbed my hand for the first time, led me down the fields, dangerously close to her home, and then down and down into the valley, over the boggy marshland and beyond a copse of thin, straggly trees, where there was a derelict barn.

My heart bashed against my rib cage as I imagined why the hell she had brought me here. Here, far away from everywhere, and she'd grabbed my hand earlier, and maybe she actually wanted to . . .

"I'm gonna run away, Shaney! It was a brilliant idea, and I'm doing it!"

Of course she didn't want to do anything like that with me.

She pushed open the wooden door to the barn and led me in. It was a smallish space with one filthy window high up on one wall, the branches of the trees knocking against the glass. There were some stones in one corner, where someone had perhaps planned to use them to build a wall but never got around to it. The walls were huge gray stones and peeling mortar, and thick wooden beams held up the walls and roof. Someone had carved *T. RILEY 1969* into one of them, and the name looked almost as old and weathered as the stones themselves.

Greta had brought a sleeping bag and some bits and had put them against the far wall. She looked at my face, trying to gauge my reaction as I realized what was happening.

"You're running away to live in a barn on your dad's land?" I asked, failing to hide the suspicion in my voice.

"Don't be stupid. I'm just hiding some stuff here now. Trying to work out what I need before I go."

And after that, every few days, we'd meet in the barn, making lists in our minds and trying to work out a plan for Greta's future. Sometimes, if it rained, we sat on the stones in the barn, listening to the rain flicking on the corrugated metal roof, but it was mostly fine weather, and we sat outside among the trees, the moss wetting the bums of our jeans and our smoke and sweets making everything taste musky and sugary.

She seemed so, so happy then.

Full of plans. She was biding her time in order to get more cash, and she couldn't take a whole lot of it without looking suspicious. She'd pretend to her parents that she'd spent her money on clothes and makeup and expensive coffees with her friends, when in reality, she was taking out cash and stashing the notes in an empty makeup bag stored in the bottom of her wardrobe.

"I've got a couple of hundred saved up already!" She grinned at me one afternoon as we sat outside the barn. She was glowing with the expectation of escape. I'd never seen her looking so utterly comfortable.

"How the hell did you get that much in a few weeks?"

"I told Dad I needed new trainers for PE. He gave me loads of money, and he's never going to ask to see them. If he does, I'll say I left them at school." She grinned. "And I've said that I'm in the end-of-term play and that I'm always at rehearsals when I'm actually with you, preparing to leave. He gives me money for snacks and dinner. He likes drama and singing and all that; he likes it when I show off."

"But he'll find out you've been lying to him when the play happens and you're not in it."

"I'll be gone by then, anyway! God, you're stupid sometimes." She shook her head and giggled, and I couldn't help it—my face broke into a smile.

She had it all planned out in her head.

The plan was this:

Once she had enough money, she'd pick a Friday and tell her parents that she had a school project on and was planning to stay with Keira so that they could work on it late. We talked about how to make it convincing so that her parents wouldn't get suspicious. She'd have to make small talk about the project, throw in a few facts about it over dinner, pretend to be annoyed that she had to be inside working on a Friday evening instead of out enjoying the dying rays of sunset.

She would say that she was going straight from school to Keira's and would then stay with her until Saturday evening.

"Why don't you tell them you're staying with her until Sunday?" I asked when she was going over the fine details with me. "That would buy you more time."

"They'd smell a rat. It's too long. I don't want them to think I'm doing anything out of the ordinary at all."

But Greta wouldn't be staying with Keira at all. She was going to skip school that day, having faked a letter saying she had a medical appointment that would take all day.

When she'd leave home that morning, it would have to seem like just another day to her parents, but she would know that it was the last time she'd ever see them, and the last time she'd ever see her home. She was going to fill her schoolbag with warm clothes and make sure that she had all her money with her. She'd thought about it and decided not to leave a hidden note for her parents. They didn't deserve an explanation, and anyway, it would be hell for them, guessing why she'd gone.

She imagined that moment so many times—yelling out, *See you!* and letting the front door crash shut behind her and smelling the fresh air outside the farmhouse, knowing that she'd never smell the clean-scented air of her home ever again.

Then she would walk down the lane in the direction of the town, jump over a gate before reaching the main road, and head for the barn. I'd be there waiting for her—of course I would—and she'd set about changing out of her uniform and into the clothes I'd bought for her with the money she had given me. She'd twist her hair up and wear it under a slouch beanie. Her big backpack—the type that travelers wear—would be all packed and ready.

We'd smoke and eat sweets for a bit, just to let the morning traffic die down. She'd leave her old phone with me—I was supposed to get rid of it—and she'd set up her new, crappy, untraceable phone. The only number she'd put into it would be mine. "You're the only one who really understands."

And then she'd go.

Over the mountain and down a narrow, steep path into a town in the next valley. It would take her most of the day, but the town was full of tourists, so she wouldn't look out of place. There, she would catch a bus to another town and then another bus to a city on the outskirts of Wales. That city had a huge railway station, and she was then going to hop on a train and go.

"Go where?" I asked when she told me, and her face shone as she answered me.

"London, maybe. I dunno. Somewhere I can get lost. And no one will know where I am!"

"You'll tell me, though, right?"

"I'll send you a message to let you know I'm safe."

None of it was necessary, and I told her so. She only had to get on a bus from Bethesda, a train from Bangor, and she could go. It wasn't like she was a little child. There was no need for hiding her hair under a cap or walking across the mountain so that no one would recognize her on the bus. "You're sixteen," I reminded her. "There isn't gonna be a manhunt. You're allowed to go."

"I don't trust them not to get CCTV footage and follow me," she replied in a small voice. I think she knew that there was something childlike and immature about the way she was planning this, all the extra steps she was taking, as if she was a hostage making a break for it. Her excitement was starting to worry me, too, as if she thought she'd get to London and a brand-new life would be there for her, waiting at the station.

"What will you do in London?" I asked.

"I'll get a job. I don't want to stay there forever—I want to go overseas."

"You only speak English and Welsh."

"Yeah, I mean to somewhere like America or Australia."

I didn't want to bring her down, but I thought I knew what kind of jobs sixteen-year-olds would get in a big city like London and what types of places they'd have to live in on the measly salaries they'd get. Even though I knew how awful Greta's life was at home, and even though I understood why she had to get away, I also knew that her life was going to go on being awful even after she left. She'd have to worry about money, when she'd never even thought about it before. She'd have times when she'd have to choose between food and warmth, and some nights, she'd be huddling under dirty sheets in a dank, gray bedsit where she didn't feel safe. I knew she'd think about Bryn Mawr then. The way the radiators were always warm, and there was always nice food in the fridge, and the whole world was open to her from that isolated, luxurious farmhouse.

She was swapping one type of misery for another, but I couldn't bring myself to tell her that. I couldn't break that beam of joy that had been radiating from her since she'd decided to run away. But I held the dread for her and didn't tell anyone. No one else knew what she was planning.

I don't know why she trusted me.

I knew what kind of life she was yearning for. She wanted to arrive on the train and book a cheap and dingy but chic hotel in Camden Town. Then she'd be grabbing a coffee the next morning and would wander through the market with the takeaway cup in her hands, enjoying all the colors and textures of the clothes on the stalls and hanging outside the shops. She'd breathe in the smell of black coffee and fried onions and incense and weed, and then she'd notice a woman standing at one of the stalls, watching her.

Greta would like her to be exactly the same age as her mother but have bluntly cut hair dyed fuchsia. Her makeup would be severe—red lips, thick black eye shadow, and pale skin lined and ridged like maps of home. She'd be wearing a leather jacket—the type with straps and buckles, heavy leather on a slight body, and a red dress underneath it. Impossible heels. And she'd look at Greta, who hadn't brought her best clothes with her, and she'd say, *I had hair like yours when I was a girl.*

They'd chat then about hair dye and makeup and clothes, and the woman—Greta wanted her to be called Viv or Cass or Betty—would ask Greta about her accent. And Greta, who was, remember, only a day or so into her new life, would say she was from North Wales but that she didn't want to specify. In fact, Greta would add, she'd only just arrived—Viv didn't happen to know of any jobs, did she? And Viv would look at her for a while, as if she was trying to strip Greta's clothes and skin and bones away so that she could see her soul. *Come and sit at the back with me,* she'd say. *Let me roll us a smoke.*

The film in Greta's mind would then cut to a month or so later. Greta would be working on that very market stall and making a roaring trade. She'd cut her hair into a blunt bob above her shoulders (her father liked her to wear her hair long) and dyed the bottom inch a cool blue. She was dressed in clothes that wouldn't have suited who she was in Bethesda—tie-dyed dresses, big bulky boots, army jackets, and brightly colored baseball caps. She'd be living with Viv, who was cool and funny but motherly, too, always telling Greta that she was too thin, always trying to push her to have another portion of homemade chips and nagging her that breakfast was the most important meal of the day.

What would happen after that was mistier in Greta's imagination—there was a chance to work in fashion and a move to New York City and money and a townhouse and success. But Greta didn't really yearn for those things in the same way she was yearning for Viv and Camden and that tie-dyed dress.

"Do you not daydream?" she asked once, when she was telling me about the exact type of clothes she'd like to be selling when she got to London, the feel of the cotton, the exact shade of the colors. She was packing her bag again, like she did whenever we visited the barn. There was absolutely no need, but I think it made running away feel more real. She'd unpack everything, fold it again, and pack it back tightly.

"Sort of," I replied, but I don't think it was the same for her and me. My daydreams were small. I might daydream about what would happen if a certain girl asked me out or if I scored a brilliant goal in a football game at school. Once or twice I'd allowed myself to daydream about what it would be like if I unexpectedly passed all my exams with flying colors, shocking all my teachers and friends and Mam. I'd thought about what it would be like to be clever enough to go to university, maybe get one of those amazing jobs where you're paid ridiculous amounts of money and you could afford anything and . . .

None of it was going to happen. I stopped myself from imagining things that were too wonderful. Why break your own heart with things that were out of your reach? It was different for Greta—nothing had ever felt out of her reach, so she'd never learned not to daydream.

"You should daydream, it's brilliant. You can have whatever life you want inside your own head!"

"It's pointless."

"Don't be so cynical, for God's sake. When I'm at home and can't sleep and everything is awful, I think about how I could be living in my own house one day and what it'll be like and what kind of curtains I'll have and what my kitchen will look like and what will be growing in the garden."

I smiled, although it wasn't funny, not really. It was sad. "Most people would be imagining and hoping for a house exactly like yours. You know that, don't you?"

"Yes, I know that. But not me. I'm imagining the shop I want to be working in in Camden, and what exactly they'll sell, and where I'll go to buy my lunch, and who'll come out to the pub with me in the evenings."

I felt a sharp jolt of jealousy when she said that, although it wasn't unreasonable of her to say it. Of course she'd be going out with people after she'd run away. Of course she'd be chatting to them, not me, about her work and her hopes. They'd probably share bags of gummy bears, and she'd take all the green ones for herself as she did with me. There would be another Shane. I was jealous of them already.

I wanted to ask her questions about me. I wanted to know how she felt about me exactly—was I a best friend? A potential boyfriend? Would she text me a lot once she had run away? Would she send me photos? Would I be allowed to come and stay with her and experience some of her new, clean, glamorous life? Or would I never hear from her again? Would I grow old never seeing Greta again?

Did she like me?

I couldn't ask any of it. I didn't feel I had the right to know the answers. She trusted me, somehow, inexplicably, although I was almost a man, and men had always let her down. If I asked her whether she liked me, she'd know that she meant something to me, and I didn't like the thought of that—as if my feelings were her responsibility and not my own. I watched her packing her clothes again, and I knew that her mind was already in London, far away from me. I would be left again, as I had been left before, and I'd be okay. People like me, we're always okay.

"It's funny." She smiled to herself. "I've imagined Viv from Camden so many times, she feels real. As if she'll actually be there when I go to London. I know what her hands look like, what her perfume's like, her voice."

"I feel like I know her, you've gone on about her so much."

"But she doesn't exist! Isn't that nuts? My mind just made her up!"

But of course her mind had conjured up this very person—a mother figure, caring, generous, loving. She was who Greta craved more than anyone else—someone whom she could relax with, someone who would care for her no matter what. It wasn't Greta's imagination that had created a vivid, exciting, safe life in London—it was her need.

Greta didn't go to London, of course. One day, she didn't turn up to meet me at the barn like she said she would. I sat in the doorway for a long time, watching the drizzle and wondering where she was. Her stuff was still in the barn, so I knew that she hadn't taken off and left for London without telling me, and I wasn't really worried. She'd probably been unable to get away from the house. Her parents might have insisted she stay, or they had unexpected visitors, something like that.

I wonder if I'll still come here when she's gone, I thought to myself, an unexpectedly sentimental thought for me. I liked the barn—it was quiet and secluded and out of everyone's way, and I could sit here alone for hours, and no one would come by; no one would know where I was. I could even make it a bit nicer, fix the hole in the roof, block the draft that came in through the window. I had no idea how to do any of that, but you could learn everything on YouTube. Maybe I could camp out here sometimes. Make a small fire outside.

I didn't hear from Greta that day, which didn't surprise me—she was afraid of messaging me because her father sometimes randomly checked her phone. She'd get in touch when she wanted to. And anyway, the next day was a school day, so I'd see her there.

As I sat in the doorway of that barn where we'd planned the rest of her life and none of mine, I listened to the quiet hiss of the rain on the leaves of the ash trees around me and wondered how any of this was fair. She was going away and getting a new life, and I was the one who had to help her. She told me everything, me and only me, but didn't like me enough to publicly be my friend. She could have told Keira and Ela that we'd been hanging out, that I was special, that we shared secrets.

They wouldn't tell her dad. But she didn't, and no one knew, and still, I kept being there for her, helping her.

Surely I deserved better. A short shock of anger pulsed through me, which was an unfamiliar feeling. Why was I putting up with her? Why did she think I should put up with her?

The anger didn't last long. I didn't allow it to. I'd never liked the feeling of anger, especially not in the way some lads my age seemed to— some of them loved to fight, loved the feeling of losing it at a referee or a teacher or a sibling. Some even went out looking for things to piss them off, hoping that something would rile them enough that they'd want to fight over it. Not me. I couldn't afford to lose control in that way.

Plus, Greta looked terrible at school the next day.

No, not terrible—she never looked terrible at school; she was all smiles and sheen and calm confidence. But she didn't look like *her*. There was something about her movements that seemed forced, some stiffness to her smile that wasn't authentic. And she didn't look up at me once, didn't catch my eye.

She didn't phone me that night.

Or the next, or the next. There were no late conversations, snatched minutes from a pay phone or the Bryn Mawr house phone, telling me to be at the barn at 6:00 p.m. or behind the wall by the woodland at 5:00. I tried not to think about it, but of course I could think of nothing else. Had something happened? Had she met another friend that she preferred to me, and was she a bit embarrassed that she'd grown so close to someone who was so different from her?

Was this what they called ghosting? Because it made *me* feel a bit like a ghost—pale and irrelevant and not really anywhere, not really.

It was eight days before she rang me. It was from a pay phone—I could hear the line beeping, her voice soft as if it was speaking from a long, long way away. "I'm sorry," she said as soon as I answered the call. "I couldn't get away to phone you until now."

"Are you okay?" I was on my bed, playing on the console, and I sat up straighter. "Do you want me to come?"

"No, it's fine. Dad's keeping a close eye on me. He found out."

"About London?"

"Just that I've been lying. It's not good, Shaney."

"How did he find out?"

"He saw a few of my teachers down at the rugby club. Found out I'm not in the school play." I should have guessed that that might have happened. It was a weak lie.

I sighed, exasperated. That bastard. I wondered what hell he'd given Greta, what kind of cage he was keeping her in. Was she grounded? Allowed her phone? Worse still, was he watching her every move, keeping her close to him, making sure that she could do nothing at all without him knowing about it?

"You could go," I said. "Go to London. You're sixteen. He can't stop you."

She was silent on the other end of the line. I wondered which phone box she was in, how she looked under the pale white light. I could imagine her slim, waxy fingers clutching the phone, her blue eyes wide at the thought of what I was saying.

"Camden Town. And . . . what was she called? Viv! She'll be there."

"I can't," Greta whispered, and I realized then that it wasn't a physical *can't* but an emotional one—she wasn't going to be able to move on from this. It was a dream he'd killed for her, somehow, and I never knew exactly what he'd said or done. Gradually, he loosened his grip on her again, and she was allowed out, allowed her phone, and we'd meet up again, still secretly. We never went to the barn again. I didn't know whether her stuff was still in there, packed up and ready to leave for a new life. After she died, part of me thought I should go there and see—but I couldn't bring myself to. I wasn't a sentimental person, not at all, but part of me liked the fact that it was all still there, waiting for Greta, a small piece of her hope that I didn't want to disturb.

CHAPTER 13

Jesus Christ, but Liz Pugh looked great on the screen.

It's a terrible thing to say about anyone, but grief suited her. She fit perfectly into the role of a broken woman, a mother who was forever changed. I would never understand how people didn't see right through her act. People from Bethesda, people who knew her. It was so clear to me that she was faking.

"You can't say something like that!" Ela gasped, askance. She was sitting on Gwyn's knee in the school hall during a rainy break time, not seeming to notice that he looked desperately uncomfortable. "She's lost her daughter! And Liz is really nice!" Ela shook her head. "What a shitty thing to say."

"I'm not saying that it's not tragic," I replied, silently noting that no one else in the group was outraged by what I'd said. "I'm not saying that she isn't upset. Just that there's a bit of acting going on, for the cameras. It's natural, isn't it; she needs to seem as gutted as possible."

"She *is* gutted!" Ela bit back.

"I'm sure she is," I replied. But I *wasn't* sure. Not at all. There was a silence between us as the noise of a wet day at school reverberated in the hall around us—someone laughing, someone swearing, someone bouncing a forbidden ball on the tiled floor.

"I've got to say . . . ," Keira ventured in a small voice.

"You're not serious!" Ela spit.

"Shane *does* have a point. Don't pretend. You know what things were like between Greta and her mother."

"Everyone argues with their parents!"

"Not like that! I know you feel for Liz and Kelvin, but this is ridiculous. Greta told you what they were like. You should still believe her, even though she's not here to remind you."

"You're so mean!" But everyone could hear a slight edge of reservation in her voice, as if the doubts were starting to take root. She hadn't allowed herself to consider it before, her sympathy toward Liz clouding everything else. Poor Ela—she seemed so normal and predictable and boring, really, but she'd always have to live with the fact that she was jealous of her murdered best friend. "Liz would never fake it! How could you even think such a thing?!"

The sound of camera shutters like the sharpening of knives. A respectful silence as DCI Call Me Karen sat beside Liz and Kelvin Pugh. That school photo of Greta in the background, her smile almost shameless, almost rude, in a room full of downcast faces.

Kelvin in jeans and a shirt (Mam had probably ironed it for him), looking as if he hadn't slept in months. He wasn't crying but somehow looked too tired and too sad to cry. He held his wife's hand on the white table in front of them, his hands red and square around her delicate white fingers. He hardly said a word in front of the cameras—just "Please tell the police if you know anything" in a thick Welsh accent, his voice ragged and rasping.

But Liz—well. Liz was different.

I'd never seen her in joggers before.

Oh, she'd been a runner for years—of course she had, that's what people like her did *to deal with stress.* Putting one foot in front of the other did nothing to solve real, actual, proper problems.

Liz always ran in the right gear—colored designer leggings, a skin-tight T-shirt, and trainers that were replaced every seven hundred miles. Otherwise, she'd wear dresses or skirts, jeans at a push if her top and heels were smart enough.

But in the weeks following Greta's death, whenever Liz was in front of a camera, she wore navy blue joggers, pumps, and a white sweater. Her hair was in a ponytail—another thing she'd never done before—and her makeup was subtle, muted. She was still pretty, but it was a quiet, unassuming kind of prettiness.

She was crying. Not big, ugly, red-nosed sobs, no graceless exclamations of pain. Just tiny pearlescent tears running prettily down her cheeks. She had to take a deep breath, steady herself before she spoke. "Um . . ." Swallowed several times, a gulp of air. It was a magnificent performance. Her audience considered her brave before she'd even uttered a word.

"Greta was my best friend" in a half whisper. Liar. She *knew* she was a liar. "I just don't know why anyone would hurt her."

Some mothers spend a lifetime torturing their children. Most of them, I think. I don't know if they do it on purpose, but they keep on doing it in huge and tiny ways for years and years, before their children become parents, and the pattern is repeated.

Some, like Ela's mother, do too much. Are *too* nice. She was Ela's friend. They went shopping together and shared clothes. They adored one another. And although it was fine for them then, pleasant even, being that close to her mother would make life difficult for Ela later on. She wouldn't be able to live with her forever, and everyone else she'd ever meet, everyone she'd ever love, would be a bit of a disappointment in comparison to her mother. She had no hope of finding anyone who loved her as much as her mam did.

Liz, on the other hand, wasn't like that at all. The damage she did was a different kind, a crueler kind. I had no idea to begin with, but once Greta started speaking to me about it, she couldn't seem to stop. And somehow, although the things Greta said were shocking, I wasn't shocked. Liz was sweet and kind and perfect, and it wasn't hard to imagine her torturing Greta.

That's what she'd speak about, more often than not, when it was just Greta and me. And Greta had a way of telling a story. She made it all play like a film in my head, and it was the kind of film your parents wouldn't want you to watch.

◆ ◆ ◆

"Don't wear that, sweetheart," Liz told her daughter with a tight smile. "It isn't flattering."

Greta looked at her mother, who in turn was staring at Greta's thighs. This was Liz's game, loaded words spoken with a smile, her eyes fixed on whichever part of Greta's body displeased her that day. Her legs. Her bum. Her belly. To us at school, Greta was stunning, but Liz only saw her flaws, all the tiny, insignificant imperfections.

"I like it," Greta said, turning to the toaster. She was trying out a new attitude. Greta had made a decision. She wasn't going to let this happen anymore. She wasn't going to change her clothes, but she wasn't going to argue either.

"Well. That's the important thing," replied Liz, a slight edge of surprise in her voice. She'd expected Greta to get changed straight away. She was used to being in control of her daughter.

"Yup," said Greta, her mind repeating a silent mantra—*Ihateyou Ihateyou Ihateyou Ihateyou.*

"There's some fruit in the fridge." Liz started to stack the glasses and mugs from the countertop into the dishwasher. "Fewer calories than toast."

Greta pulled out the hot toast from the toaster even though she would have liked it a bit darker. She opened the cupboard where the spreads were kept, the jam and marmalade and honey and Marmite. Poor Greta—she was so familiar with the hot bubble of rage growing in her guts that she knew she was horribly close to screaming or crying. She clenched her teeth hard, determined to keep her mouth shut. She pulled out two jars—the chocolate spread and the peanut butter because they were the ones with the most calories.

She felt her mother's eyes watching her.

Greta spread the chocolate ridiculously thick on the two slices of toast—she used up almost one-quarter of the jar—and then added the peanut butter in fat, crunchy globules. It didn't look very appetizing, but that wasn't the point.

Greta licked the knife.

She lifted a slice of toast to her mouth and took a huge bite, raising her eyes to meet her mother's as she chewed. Liz stared at her in complete silence, a strange half smile on her pretty face.

"You make me sick," she said to her daughter.

"Piss off," Greta replied, her syllables like bullets across the kitchen.

It killed Greta, all of this. She used to sit there in the shade of the hedges or the walls or on one of the long, smooth slates of the quarry, and she'd list for me all the mean things her mother had told her. Sometimes they were cruel, and sometimes they were torturous.

You could always put padding in your bra . . .

Not everyone can be naturally clever . . .

I do feel for you, with skin like that . . .

Yes, but a size eight now is the equivalent to a twelve ten years ago . . .

It must be difficult for you, what with having a best friend as gorgeous as Keira . . .

And on and on and on. One thing after the other, one failure after another, until the most popular girl in our class felt like an ogre.

But the final time was the worst. Greta and I, the Tuesday before she died. We had met up at the very top of the quarry because it was sunny and people were still using the zip line to zoom down the mountain. Every now and then, their screams would bounce off the slates and boom an echo around us.

"I bought you this," I said, throwing a bag of gummy bears at Greta. She caught it and smiled weakly. She was clearly broken again—something big this time, something terrible. This was worse than when she cried. "What's up?"

"Mam," she sighed. "And Dad, I think. Oh, Shaney, I'm crappy company, aren't I? Always moaning about something."

"Yeah, you're awful," I agreed with a tiny smile. "What's happened?"

"Sometimes," she replied softly, "I think that those two could hurt me, you know. I mean, really hurt me."

She didn't tell me everything. That could feel worse, because when I didn't have the facts, my imagination filled in the blanks. There's nothing as bad as the things your mind can cook up.

The argument between Liz and Kelvin had been awful. Really, properly awful, said Greta—wineglasses thrown across rooms, a wedding photograph pulled from its frame and torn in two. The cruelest, crudest words imaginable thrown across that expensive designer kitchen in their grand, luxurious house. Liz had been unfaithful again—*again*—said Greta, her nonchalance after a lifetime lived like this repulsive to me. In another house at the other end of the valley, another middle-aged couple—Liz and Kelvin's best friends until that night—were having the same argument. No one else would ever know, of course, but Kelvin knew. And now, Greta knew too. She hid in her bedroom, jammed her headphones in, and turned up the volume. She texted her friends about anything but this, bitching about their teachers, as something else was smashed into shards in the kitchen.

Kelvin burst into her room, tears streaking down his face. He had been drinking, but it wasn't the wine that was making him weep. "She's a fucking psychopath, Gret . . . please. Please help me!"

Greta pulled out her headphones and stared up at her father. "I can't . . ."

And that's when Liz strode in. She wasn't beautiful now, but twisted, her face warped by anger and made grotesque, her eyes flashing.

In that moment, Greta wished she was brave enough to pick up her phone and take a photo of her mother to share on her social media accounts. The Real Liz.

If she had been brave enough to do that, the murder case might have been a very different one. Perhaps someone else would be languishing in jail.

Liz stared at Kelvin and then at Greta, the silence thick and dangerous. "How the hell can *you* have a go at *me* for being unfaithful?"

She turned to her daughter, and as Greta told me later, there was nothing but poison in that stare. "You ruined everything."

"What a bitch!" I told Greta as we sat on the slate, watching the fools glide down the zip line. I didn't ask what Liz meant when she'd said that about Kelvin being unfaithful. That question felt too big.

"She's a monster." Greta opened the bag of sweets and crammed her hand inside. "God knows what she'll do next."

"You could run away," I said, the horror of the scene she'd just narrated for me slowly gaining color and shape inside my head. It was horrific, a film I'd never be able to unsee. "London."

"I don't have faith in that plan anymore," she answered, a devastatingly simple, sad truth that I knew wouldn't change.

"Tell someone. Tell a teacher!"

"Do you remember Mary? And that horrible art teacher?"

"Yeah . . ."

"She told, didn't she? Look what happened there."

And I wanted to argue with her about it, wanted to say it would be different with her, and that if either of her parents had done anything illegal, the police would *have* to listen, and that anyway, she was sixteen, they couldn't control her anymore.

But I knew she'd argue. I knew she felt helpless and hopeless, and the more answers I came up with, the more reasons she'd find to carry on with things as they were.

"Who the hell did I think I was, running away?" she said lightly, with a sad smile. "As if I could just *go*. As if I could leave everybody like that and never look back."

"Well, you could. Or you could go for a while and then come back when you're older. When your parents don't have as much control."

She looked over, and I saw a blank sheen in her eyes. I think I lost a part of our friendship when I said that, although I didn't realize it at the time. She must have known that with all my tragic background, my broken family, and faraway sharp, stinging memories, I would never understand that she couldn't just escape. Couldn't get away from their control just by moving away.

She looked away from me, the rain spitting on her face. She never looked so beautiful.

CHAPTER 14

One day, we went away.

Just Greta and me. Not far, but far enough. When I think back about it, it feels like a chapter from a different book.

I wish the whole story was like that one chapter.

It was six months or so before she died, and she seemed to be living on the tides then, not quite settled, not quite right. I didn't think of it much at the time, but she had a certain fizzing energy about her, tapping her pen on her schoolbook in class, looking around all the time as if someone might walk in any moment. It was almost as if she was waiting for something to happen, but maybe it was just waiting for her own life.

It had been my birthday. Just another ordinary Thursday, but that morning, the sun streamed through the curtains I'd forgotten to draw the night before, and the droplets of condensation on the window looked like tiny pearls. Mam had bought me Pop-Tarts for breakfast as a treat, and I got a new T-shirt with the logo of my favorite band and trainers and a color-changing lamp for my room. She'd baked a cake, too, a chocolate cake with an *S* made out of M&M's pressed into the icing.

Although you wouldn't have guessed it about me, I loved birthdays. It was a feeling left over from my childhood, I think, when Mam had worked extra hard to battle the fact that we had no money to make me feel special. There had always been Pop-Tarts and a funny birthday card with a silly face of an animal on it. She had always baked me cakes—train-shaped ones and Spider-Man ones, ones in the shape of game consoles and football fields, and recently, more elegant ones with my favorite sweets and chocolates dotting the tops. I had a few birthday parties at home when I was a young child, until the kids got too big and the house too small. After that, Mam made a tradition of taking me to Rhyl on my birthday. We'd go on the train and eat delicious, unhealthy food, and I'd get five pounds to spend, and we'd buy comics to read on the way home. It was childish, but even as I got older, we'd go to Rhyl on the weekend of my birthday, wander around as if we were on holiday, feel naive again. I'd outgrown the comics, and we'd stared at our phones instead, but it was still an occasion. It still felt special.

And of course it had stopped a few years before, because traditions do die in the end, and it would have felt weird, being a teenager and celebrating by going shopping with my mother. I don't think we ever mentioned the fact that we'd stopped, but Mam gave me the money she would have spent on the trip, and our celebrations became more muted—a film on TV, something nice to drink, and a fish supper with all the trimmings. Cake and more cake for dessert.

"So how are you celebrating?" asked Greta, her face dim in the twilight. It was the day after my birthday, and we were eating gummy bears in the shadow of a stone wall on the mountain.

"We had fish and chips last night. I might go to Bangor tomorrow, spend my money."

"That sounds crap," she said, her forehead puckering. "It just sounds like a normal weekend."

"We only have fish and chips on birthdays," I replied, and she nodded and licked the sugar off her lips thoughtfully, silently, as if she'd said something wrong. But she was in a good mood, uncharacteristically laid back, and I didn't want to sour things. "We used to go to Rhyl when it was my birthday. Every year."

Greta looked up at me and chuckled a deep, throaty giggle. "Rhyl? Why Rhyl?"

"I dunno. It's far enough away to feel like a big trip. You never see anyone you know there. And it's nice."

"Is it, now?" she said doubtfully, her mouth still twisted into a smile.

"Yes! It has a funfair and amusements and little shops that sell everything. And a beach! And ice cream."

"Sounds great." Greta dug her fingers into the bag of sweets, pincering a handful. "We should go."

I hesitated. "Yeah." I knew she didn't mean it. She said things like that sometimes, as people did—made half promises about the future that would never happen, like *We'll have to go for a coffee* or *You'll have to come over sometime.* And I just agreed, because I knew she didn't mean it, but I didn't want to call her out on it.

"Tomorrow," she said. "We could go tomorrow. It's Saturday. We'll go on the train, sit separately until we're far enough away. Just in case Dad finds out."

"What?" I sat up straighter, a buzz of adrenaline daring to hope that she did mean it after all. "You serious?"

Greta shrugged her shoulders. "Sure. Why not?"

And I could have pushed her. I could have replied, *Because we never go anywhere public together* and *Because I've never had you for a whole Saturday* and *Because you probably have better people to be spending your time with.* But I wanted to go. I wanted to go with Greta. "There's a train at ten past ten from Bangor."

"Ace," she said, drinking the sugar from the bottom of the bag. "You bring the sweets."

◆ ◆ ◆

Rhyl was only thirty miles from Bethesda, and a thousand miles too. Our small town was planted deep in the valley, protected and shadowed by the mountains, their craggy peaks stabbing toward a sky that was often gray and heavy with the promise of rain. We had greenery everywhere, mossy woodlands with paths like veins, leading everywhere, always with the promise of silence and stillness and a profound, ancient beauty.

Rhyl was shrill.

Down on the coast, the busy main carriageway led away from the mountains and toward the flatlands. Villages and towns dotted the seaside, getting bigger as the road neared the English cities of Manchester and Liverpool, holiday places for those who were fed up with city life. Rhyl was the capital of the North Wales seaside towns.

It was garish and loud and raw and real, and I loved it. I loved its tired funfair with its rickety roller coaster and peeling paint, loved the amusement arcades with their lights flashing like fat precious jewels. I loved the bold, thieving seagulls that hung around outside the burger joints and the ice cream parlors, ready to swoop in gracefully.

Greta hadn't been before.

She looked around as we walked from the station toward the town center, at the tired café with the fading sign, and the crumbling Victorian plaster on the row of houses we passed, and the way the watery-blue sky peeked between the buildings. She was wearing a puffer jacket and a black baseball cap, almost a disguise, and no makeup, but even dressed down, Greta looked amazing. She had the look of money about her, a nameless, unspecific thing that couldn't be faked.

It felt odd, walking around in public with her. People looked. She didn't seem to notice. I felt proud and unworthy. I wondered if people thought we were together.

It was the best birthday celebration I ever had.

At the amusement arcades, we played a shooting game, and I absolutely pulverized her, and then she decided to take it seriously and beat me twice. She spent twenty pounds trying to win a pig-shaped soft toy in a claw machine, even though I'd told her that it was rigged and that she was never going to get it. And we spent a full hour on the twopence machines, the ones that fed the coins onto a shelf with a metal arm that pushed all the money into a teetering pile at the edge. She loved those machines, loved spending all her money and then winning it all back in a jubilant crash of coins and then having to spend it all again because who wanted to walk around with a load of twopence pieces?

I was having such a good time that I barely even looked at her. Just heard her screeching laughter at the machine beside mine, her occasional frustrated swearing, her giggle as she reached into my pot of money for a twopence piece. I forgot that she was Greta and I was just Shane.

As we walked out of the amusement arcade, blinking in the brightness of the daylight, she put her fingers up to my nose and said, "Smell the money on me." The coins had left a rusty, bloodish scent on her hands.

We were the only ones who rode on the roller coaster, and she grabbed my hand in real terror as the car slowly climbed to the ascent: "Yeah, but it could really break, couldn't it, Shane; we could really fall off; this place is all so wonky, and it could crack, and I don't want to die!" And I didn't feel odd that she was holding my hand—there was no frisson of excitement, no thrill of electricity, because it was normal. She screamed when the car finally dropped down the steep track and looped the loop, swearing in a joyful, terrified way that made me laugh out loud. We collapsed into the ghost-train car after that because her knees felt weak and she wanted to sit down.

"We could have actually died," she said as the doors opened and our car moved jerkily into the ride.

"No way," I replied. "They test these things all the time. You never really hear of people dying on them." A plastic ghost covered in fake cobwebs swung down before us. We ignored it. There was off-key piano music playing in the background, like some awful ghostly cartoon.

"They probably cover up the deaths," Greta said confidently, readjusting her cap.

"Don't be ridiculous."

"They do! We almost died just now." She grinned at the thought. "Imagine if we had died! What would people say at school?"

I looked over at her, trying to guess what she was thinking. "They'd have thought I was mad, coming out to celebrate my birthday with a munter like you." I nudged her playfully, and Greta giggled as a vampire lit up beside us, blood dripping from his fangs and the paint cracking on his black hair. A light flickered in a corner, showing a figure hanging by a noose from a lamppost.

"Gross," she said, shaking her head. "He's barely human shaped. I wonder how they made him?"

The ghost train wandered slowly from tired werewolf to shoddy banshee, and Greta and I simply looked at them in mild amusement. They were terrible but not in the way that they were meant to be.

"That's your boyfriend," I teased as we passed a molting yeti, whose paw was jerking up and down in a way that was meant to be threatening. Greta released a burst of laughter before turning to a gaggle of three witches with plastic faces, crouched around a dusty polystyrene cauldron.

"Wow, look, your exes, all together, probably chatting shit about you."

I laughed. The ghost train moved through a graveyard of cardboard gravestones and fake cobwebs, and Greta and I insulted one another cheerfully and giggled. By the time the train reached the end of the ride, we were belly laughing. The man who was running the ride shook his head at us as we got out of the car.

"It's not scary, is it," he said flatly. Greta shook her head.

"You should just stop the ride for five minutes in the middle and switch off the lights," she said. "Leave people in the dark."

The man looked at Greta and nodded, but he looked unsure and a bit unnerved at her suggestion.

"Or," she added with a cheerful smile, "get the bodies of the people who have died on the roller coaster and prop them around the place. That'll freak people out."

The smile slid off the man's face, although he was still nodding. I bit back my laughter as we walked away.

"Prop up the bodies?" I said under my breath. "What the hell's wrong with you?"

"Well it *would* be scary!"

Greta was somebody else that day.

Her laugh was different, a huge, blaring, unselfconscious guffaw that drew the looks and smiles of passersby. Her walk was lighter, more energetic. She was *fun*, in a way that I didn't know she was capable of being.

It was raining lightly through the sun as we walked on the promenade, the beach a band of gold as blonde as her hair, stretching out toward a deep blue sea, and dozens of wind turbines on the horizon, their stems planted deep in the ocean.

"I'm gonna get us hot dogs," Greta said, pulling my sleeve toward a tired-looking burger-and–hot dog hut, the woman behind the counter staring at her phone and blowing clouds of blueberry-scented air from her e-cigarette.

"We'll go somewhere else," I said, thinking that this place wasn't Greta's style. "Come on."

"You said when you were little, you and your mam would come to Rhyl and get hamburgers or hot dogs as a treat. For your birthday."

I blushed then, embarrassed that I'd shared the memory. "That was ages ago . . ."

"Two hot dogs, please," Greta ordered. "And I'll have onions, too, and ketchup. D'you want onions, Shaney?"

"Of course I don't want onions. Who has onions?" And the woman in the hut smiled to herself, listening to us playfully argue. I supposed she thought we were together. I supposed that to a lot of the strangers who saw us together that day, we looked like we were flirting.

We walked down the prom, eating our hot dogs, which were hot and savory and steaming and delicious. I tried not to look at Greta because I didn't want her to feel self-conscious, but I could see her out of the corner of my eye. She was taking huge bites out of her food, chomping down with no grace at all, and I smiled to myself as I remembered the way she ate her lunch at school—small, ladylike bites, tearing little pieces off her sandwich and nibbling on them, as if having an appetite was unfeminine. She finished her hot dog before me, and after she swallowed and brushed the crumbs off her hand, she let out a loud, proud belch. I laughed, shocked that someone like her could be so wonderfully bad mannered.

"That was lovely." She belched again and grinned at me. "That burp tasted like onions."

"Wow, you're actually disgusting." I smiled at her with my mouth open, showing the chewed up remains of bread and meat.

"Thanks. Right back atcha."

"You've got ketchup on your chin."

Greta paused and tilted her face toward me, waiting for me to clean her. I wetted my thumb in my mouth and wiped off the ketchup before sucking it away. It was an intimate and easy move, and I wondered whether Greta felt that, too—if it felt like we were closer, now, today.

We walked.

"So how come you used to come to Rhyl with your mam on your birthdays? Don't most kids have parties or go bowling with their mates or something?"

I planted my fists deep into my coat pockets, not particularly wanting to be reminded of real life, that we had homes and families and histories waiting for us in the crevice of the valley at home.

"We don't have money, do we." My voice sounded flat, expressionless. A bit like my voice when I was at school or with my friends. Giving nothing away.

She was silent for a bit and then said softly, "Sorry."

"It's okay. It's nothing to apologize about, is it; it's just as it is."

"We never really talk about you, do we, Shane? It's always my stuff."

I shrugged. "There isn't much to say. I get bored talking about me."

"But I remember, when we were little, at play school—all that stuff with your dad . . ."

And if there was a time for me to talk about it, it would have been then and there, with her. Far from home, when we didn't quite feel like us, and I felt safe, holding Greta's secrets and knowing I'd never share them. In Rhyl, we were perfect.

But I'd never talk about my father, not even with her. Ever.

"That was a long, long time ago," I said, hoping that she'd know not to push it. "It's just me and Mam now."

"She seems really nice. I mean, I don't know her. But when I see her, she seems kind." *Not like my mother.* She didn't even have to say it—I knew what she meant.

"Yeah, she is. I really like my mam. I mean, I really love her." I felt Greta looking at me then, surprised, and I returned her look. "What?"

"No, I mean that's really lovely. That you would say that. Most boys our age complain about their parents."

"There's nothing to complain about. She's nice."

And I told Greta about my mam. I told her about the way she worked all day cleaning people's houses, and how sometimes they'd be really filthy and they hadn't even flushed their toilets, and that Mam would be expected to deal with that all the time without complaining. And I said about how clever she was, how she read books from the library, and when she told me about them, she sounded cleverer than any of our teachers. I told Greta about how Mam would put the heating on but would switch off all the radiators except the one in my room, and she'd sleep in pajamas and a fleece with two duvets because it was too expensive to heat her room too.

"Bloody hell," said Greta. I don't think she knew that anyone lived like us, never mind most people.

"And from September, she saves up to get us Christmas treats like mince pies and chocolates and all that. But she always buys two of everything and gives one to the food bank." I didn't add that the reason Mam did that was because a few years ago, we had to use the food bank twice a week and that when Christmas came, they had bags for us, filled with boxes of mince pies and nice pop and chocolates and biscuits. Mam felt like she was paying back the favor every year by giving, even though we didn't really have the money and we rarely used the food bank now.

"You're so lucky," Greta said, snapping me out of my memories, and for a second I was confused—lucky for using the food bank? "Having a mother like that. I think you're a lot like her."

"I dunno about that. I hope so." I looked down at my feet as I walked, feeling odd. I didn't like the fact that I'd just shared so much about myself, about my life. Not that any of it was that interesting, but it was all I had, and it felt sacred.

"You know what they say. Money can't buy you happiness." She dug her fists deep into her coat pockets. "I know it's a stupid cliché, but I think it's true."

Poor Greta. She'd never understand.

Money couldn't buy you happiness, but it could buy a home and a bed and make that house and bed warm and inviting. Money could buy food for yourself and food for other people that you loved and wanted to look after. Money meant that you could afford university and holidays and a school uniform. And money could buy rides on ghost trains and roller coasters, and crappy hot dogs. Of course money could make you happy. That's what it was for.

But that day in Rhyl wasn't the time to tell Greta any of this, because it was as close to perfect as possible, and I didn't want to remind her of how different we were at a time when we both seemed to be so wonderfully similar. On the way back to the railway station, we looked in a few charity shops, and she tried on posh hats to make me laugh, and I found some nice jeans for myself, and she started leafing through an old family Bible that had been discarded, the slanting, old-fashioned handwriting of its previous owner marking the first page. She ran her thumb over the signature and smiled. "I should buy it," she said. "Save it. But I don't think it would suit being in our house." She put it back on the shelf, and I'd regret for the rest of my life the fact that I didn't buy it for her.

We sat separately on the train home, in case anyone saw us, in case anyone decided to report back to her father. But she was on the same carriage—I could see her black baseball cap from my seat. I wondered if she'd enjoyed the day as much as I had. I wondered if she'd meant it when she'd said on the station platform, "I love Rhyl. I'll never forget us here." And I wondered whether she, like me, felt a knot of hardness tightening in her belly as she approached home, as if it wasn't quite safe, wasn't quite right.

On that day in Rhyl, there were no clues about what was to come, no evidence of any impending tragedy. She didn't tell me any new secrets, and we didn't fall out or fall in love. But to me, that memory was evidence, important evidence of who Greta was. On that day, she was truly herself—nerdy, funny, unselfconscious. She wasn't trying, and she wasn't suffering. And after she died, I wished that people had known that she could be that way, but of course they didn't. I was the only one that really knew her like that.

The train trudged its way from the flatlands of the coast into the dark folds of the mountains, and my mind returned to the shadows too. I knew I'd lost the real Greta as soon as she sat away from me on that train, silently mouthing, "I'm sorry" as she fetched her headphones to drown out the sound of the journey home. But at least I'd had her. At least I'd known her.

CHAPTER 15

Poor Keira.

Because she was the best of us all, really. She was hard, of course, but always fair and always kind. She was the one who'd just say plainly when someone was behaving badly. Both Ela and Greta had copped it a few times from her for tiny things, and we boys were regularly put in our places. Things like "Stop being competitive; you look like a nob" or "Stop bitching, girls; there's a girl code, and we've got to stick together."

I remember . . .

Well. Anyway. Keira. Hard as nails, but there was a softness to her, and that combination was what made her so good, so sweet.

And Kelvin knew that.

She didn't go and stay overnight at Bryn Mawr very often. For one thing, it wasn't practical, because it was too far away from the village. But also, even though Keira and Greta had been best friends since play school, Keira wasn't sure about Greta's family. Nothing specific but enough for her to prefer it when Greta came to stay at hers.

But about three weeks before Greta died, Keira accepted an invitation to sleep over at Bryn Mawr. It was raining too much for the gang to go out to the park, and Keira's mother was having a few friends over, so her house was a bit crammed. So for once, Keira went over to Greta's.

Everyone in the gang knew this because Ela had moaned that she couldn't go because she had to visit her grandmother. She was jealous,

I think, that Greta and Keira were having an evening without her. Ela was the kind of girl who'd go on about it for a good while too.

But I didn't know what had happened that night, and I didn't get to know about it for some time after Greta's death.

It was your average type of sleepover. Bad horror films, the kind where blonde girls are viciously murdered by psychopaths in the middle of nowhere. The girls were only half watching—Greta was painting her nails, and Keira was playing a game on her phone. They chatted about everything—about us, probably, and school and work and the people we knew. Keira told me later, much later, about how Greta had started to bitch about Ela.

"She gets on my nerves," she said, carefully painting her toenails. It was a light baby pink, the color of baby onesies and candy floss. A child's color.

"Why?"

"This whole thing with Gwyn is so pathetic. Pretending she doesn't like him, even to us. Why doesn't she just say?"

"She's just shy . . . yes!" Keira had killed a monster in her game.

"I just . . . I dunno. She feels a bit . . . year eight. Don't you think?"

Keira sighed. "Stop bitching. She's sound. D'you talk about me behind my back too?"

"As if!" Greta smiled at her, and Keira playfully gave her the finger. Both were in their pajamas—Greta's were silky and pink, of course, with pictures from *Beauty and the Beast* all over them. She looked so young. "You're the best."

"Yeah, okay," replied Keira suspiciously.

"Hey, seeing as you're the best, do me a favor. Get me another Coke from the kitchen."

"Sod off! Get your own."

"Oh, go oooon. My nails are still wet, and I don't want to smudge them." And Keira, because she was kind and motherly and pretty obedient, got up and did as she was told.

It was late—almost eleven—and the only light that was on in the kitchen was the little one above the stove. Keira hurried over to the massive fridge and fetched two cans of Coke.

That's when Kelvin walked in.

He had been drinking, Keira thought—Greta's parents were wine snobs, the type of people who would sneer at anyone drinking beer while pretending that their own two-bottles-of-malbec-a-night habit was not an alcohol problem. Kelvin stood in the doorway, a beaming smile on his face. Keira smiled back stiffly. She didn't like men.

"You're still up! I thought I heard voices."

"Just fetching drinks," replied Keira, and Kelvin nodded.

"D'you want something else? We've got chocolate here somewhere . . ."

"We've had loads, thanks."

At this point, Keira would have left with a polite nod, but of course Kelvin was standing in her way. They both stood in an awkward silence for a moment, Kelvin still smiling.

"You've grown so much, Keira."

That's when Keira's heart sank.

When she explained to me what had happened that night, she told me a bit more than just the bare facts of that evening. She told me how women know when a man is going to try his luck, because they've heard it a thousand times before. Even when they're only Keira's age. *You've grown. You're a woman now! You've blossomed. You look so much older than your age! If I was twenty years younger . . .* These are all the words of dirty old men. They always mean that the girl will have to work her way out of a situation that they never wanted to be in in the first place.

"If I was twenty years younger . . . ," Kelvin said and took a step toward Keira, taking the cans out of her hands. "Do you want glasses for these?"

If he touches me, I'll knee him in the balls, Keira thought, and said, "No thanks, it's fine. Good night."

She reached for the cans, but for a short moment, Kelvin wouldn't let them go. He looked her in the eye, and—this was the worst part,

Keira told me later—he looked down at her breasts, without attempting to cover up what he was doing, and then looked up again to gauge her shock.

The living room door squeaked; Kelvin let go of the cans and stepped back from Keira. When Liz came in, she was yawning, her hair a little untidy and her makeup beginning to smudge around her eyes.

"All right, Keira?" she asked without looking. She didn't notice any unusual atmosphere between her husband and her daughter's best friend, thank goodness—she was too drunk and too tired. She just padded over to the fridge to fetch more wine.

"Fine, thanks." Keira impressed herself—her voice revealed nothing of how she was feeling.

Kelvin wandered over to his wife and put his arms around her. Liz relaxed into him straight away, wrapped her arms around his waist, and they stood there for a while, completely still and entwined.

"Sorry, Keira—I don't know what's come over him!" She could hear the smile in Liz's voice.

"Good night," said Keira, feeling as uncomfortable as Kelvin had intended her to.

"What have I done to deserve this?" Liz sighed happily, loving the rare moment of attention from her husband. She had her back turned to Keira, and Kelvin stared at the young woman—his daughter's best friend—as he ran his hands down his wife's body, feeling the shape of her.

"You're just so sexy," he said, his hands on his wife but his eyes stuck tightly on Keira.

◆ ◆ ◆

"Greta's dad is a perv," I said to Keira when she told me this over the phone. "I already knew that—he tried it on with Mam."

"Prick," Keira spit, and I could imagine her face as she thought about that, her little heart-shaped mouth puckered up and tight as a fist. "It's not about sex, though. He was doing it because he wanted to see me suffer. He likes that power."

"Jesus," I sighed. How the hell did women cope with all the bad men in the world?

"And with your mam, too . . . he knew he was putting her in an awkward position, didn't he, what with her being the cleaner. It's not that he's horny, Shane; it's that he likes the control."

I was silent. I didn't know what to say—I almost wanted to apologize on his behalf, to try and defend all the good men out there, like me. But that would have been ridiculous.

"But that's not why I told you this," Keira went on. "There's something I've been thinking about, and I'm wondering whether I should tell the cops . . ."

"What?"

"It's what Greta said afterward . . ."

Keira went back to Greta's bedroom with the Cokes. Greta was leaning into the mirror by then, tweezers in her hand, plucking stray hairs from the arches of her brows.

"The film's finished. Put another one on," she said without looking up. Keira obeyed, finding a film about a serial killer, then sat down on the carpet, trying to seem normal. But she didn't feel normal. Kelvin had made her feel guilty, as if she had done something very wrong.

Greta asked her if everything was okay, said she was quiet. "Just tired," said Keira, but those girls had been friends from the very beginning. Greta knew that there was something. And although Keira tried to be herself, because this wasn't Greta's fault, it was difficult.

When they were both in bed, the lights off, Keira in the rollaway bed and Greta in the big bed, Greta asked again. "You're okay, right? It's really not like you to be so quiet."

"I'm fine. Stop worrying!"

8

8

The silence stretched between them, no sound but the wind tripping down from the quarry and trying to break in through the thick farmhouse walls. Keira thought that Greta had fallen asleep when her voice whispered, soft as a ghost, across the darkness.

"It was Dad, wasn't it?"

◆ ◆ ◆

"She knew." Keira's voice was low and dark over the phone. "She knew what he was like. She must have done."

"What did you say?"

"Nothing. I didn't reply. Just pretended to sleep, but I think she probably knew that I was awake."

My thoughts stumbled over each other. What did it mean? *It was Dad, wasn't it?* What did Greta think he'd done?

"Should I tell the cops, Shane?"

"Why are you asking me?"

"Because you're so quiet. And you get it. I know you do. And I don't want to point a finger, you know? But he's a perv, isn't he, and they should probably know that."

I was about to tell Keira that it's never a good idea to share anything with the cops. That it was their job to find things out, not our job to give them information they were too stupid to find out for themselves.

But slowly, the pieces fell into place in my mind. Oh, this was *perfect*.

"Tell them, then. But don't phone them specially. You don't want to make a big deal of things on a weekend, do you?"

"Should I wait until school, then, d'you think?"

It was a Saturday afternoon. That left plenty of time.

"That's what I'd do."

And because I'm cunning, and because I'm a liar and a master of manipulation, I pushed it one step too far. I didn't like lying to Keira. I didn't get any of the thrill I usually got from getting away with dishonesty. Keira was a kind girl, but the truth would hurt her too much.

"Do you reckon he did it, Keira? Greta's dad?"

"Killed her?" Keira's voice rose a bit from its usual monotone. "No! No way. He thought the world of her!"

"I thought that too. But I don't know anymore. We don't know the half of it, do we?"

She was silent, and I knew that she wouldn't sleep that night, trying to work it all out. The seed was planted.

CHAPTER 16

"D'you wanna go somewhere? Bangor, maybe?"

Mam looked up at me, her lips slightly parted. She'd been scrolling on her phone in the kitchen after clearing away the breakfast dishes, and she hadn't expected this from me.

"Eh?"

"Don't look at me like that! I was only asking!"

Mam raised one eyebrow. "Have you hit your head or something?"

"Fine! We won't go, then!"

I strode out of the kitchen, knowing that she'd follow me.

She followed me.

"Is everything okay, Shane?"

I sat on the sofa and sighed. "Yeah. Just . . . you know, the whole Greta thing."

Mam sat down in the armchair, waiting for more.

"I was always a bit jealous, you know."

Mam nodded. She understood.

"She had everything. That big house and a massive room and holidays and nice clothes . . ."

"I was in school with her mother, remember," Mam replied. "Liz was the same. And I was jealous of her, even though I knew that my parents always tried their best."

"But it's all crap, isn't it? Because she doesn't have anything now. She wasn't really better than us, was she?"

"Well, I'm definitely not jealous of Liz anymore," said Mam, look-ing exhausted. "She's got all that money, and none of it will bring back her little girl."

An unusual silence filled the space between us, as if there was always infinitely more to say.

"I'm glad you're my mother." Mam turned her eyes to me, sur-prised. "Don't look at me like that. Greta's parents are a mess. And the other parents aren't much better, really; they're either obsessed with making more money or they live for the weekends or they're in denial about the fact that their kids aren't kids anymore. And you're not like that."

"Oh, Shane."

"Don't get soppy. I was just thinking, I've got nothing on, and I thought maybe we could go for a walk or go into town or something. I've got some birthday money left over . . ."

"Oh, I'd love to, sweetheart, but I'm going to Greta's house to clean today. They've asked for Saturdays, too, now, just for the moment. It's because they're getting so many visitors."

"Oh!" I made sure that I sounded the exact amount of disap-pointed. (I'd looked in her phone earlier, when she was in the shower, and had seen the word *Liz* in her cleaning schedule for today. I'd known what her plans were for hours.) "You won't be long, though, right? We could do something later."

"I'll be a good few hours . . ."

"Well . . . d'you want me to come with you? To help? We won't take long together . . ."

"I dunno, Shaney. It's not a nice place to be, not now after everything."

"Okay. It's fine; I'll do something with Dion."

"Okay . . ." Mam paused, as I knew she would. If there was one thing I could depend on, it was the fact that Mam would want to spend time with me. "Oh, sod it, yeah, go on, then. Come with me. You could hoover the bedrooms while I do the kitchen and bathrooms. Bedwyr doesn't know one end of a toilet brush from the other."

"Okay! And then we'll go somewhere."

"Thanks, Shaney."

"'S okay."

Of course Mam was foolish not to question the fact that all of a sudden, her teenage son was interested in spending time with her—interested enough to help her clean the house of people he despised. And I shouldn't have lied, not to her. Not to my mam. But I had no choice. She wasn't stupid, my mother, but all mothers are a bit stupid when it comes to their children. It's so easy to use their own love against them. More than anything else in the world, they just want to spend time with their own children.

I'd never met a woman like Mam.

I don't think that anyone else saw it. To other people, she looked so normal—a woman under forty who looked forty-five. Had always lived in the same village. Had completed half a hair-and-beauty course in college in Bangor, until she became pregnant with me and gave it up.

A dead sister. A dead mother, too, who had smoked until the very end even though the cancer in her lung was smothering her from the inside. A father who had left years ago for a cruel, unstable, sexy woman. And then there was all that business with the worst man—my own father—who damaged my mother in complex, creative ways before he did the kindest thing he ever did for her and moved away.

What people didn't know about my mother was that she wasn't the woman in shapeless, colorless clothes, the woman without makeup, the woman who carefully polished the dirt from the dark corners of the grandest houses for less than the minimum wage. Things had happened to her. They had no idea. Even I didn't know the half of it, but I knew enough.

And what you don't know is that there are so many people like Mam, people for whom getting out of bed and living a normal life are acts of heroism.

Sometimes, she was so much fun. When we watched *Friday Night Dinner* or *Father Ted* together, she laughed until she snorted. Or when she was in a good mood, she pretended to be on a cookery program while she made dinner. ". . . aaaand you just pour the beans on the toast—not all over it, you want the crusts to be crunchy and not soggy . . ." And I tried not to laugh because it was so silly and I'd heard it a hundred times before, but I couldn't help myself because she was funny and I was so, so fond of her when she was like that. Sometimes, I could see who she really was, or who she might have been—happy, contented, relaxed.

Yes. I had only asked Mam to spend time with me so that I could go to Bryn Mawr. No. I wouldn't have done it otherwise.

But I want you to understand one thing. I meant everything I said to my mother, and I'm glad I said it. She *was* better than the other parents. I *was* glad she was my mother, even though that meant I was poor, and because of that, there were so many things I wasn't able to do in my life. When you've got poor parents, you've failed before you're born.

While we were driving to Bryn Mawr, silent beside one another in the tiny car, we passed Mary. She was walking on the stretch of road between the shops and her home, a bag of shopping in her hand, hunched over like someone who had lived too many hopeless years.

I thought about the way she'd been hurt, and the way no one had been punished. I thought about the way I always kind of felt like I knew her, even though I didn't really, and whether that was a terrible effect of knowing she'd suffered. Maybe everyone had a nagging feeling that they should say hello to Mary when she passed, should offer her a tiny sad smile—though, as far as I knew, nobody ever did.

Liz was the only one who was home that afternoon, and she was happy for me to help Mam with the cleaning. She barely looked at me at all, and I felt uncomfortable looking at her, not really wanting to see grief that close up. All the things Greta had told me about her had made me despise her, but I was afraid that I'd start to pity her if I looked at her face. She looked like hell—a migraine, she said—and she said that everyone had gone out to give her some peace. She was going to bed, and could we please give their bedroom a miss today?

All of this, she said to Mam. Maybe she was as afraid of looking at me as I was of looking at her.

Mam was a good worker; that much was obvious. She did a bit of tidying in the bedrooms before fetching me the hoover, and she worked like a machine, knowing exactly where everything was meant to go. It was strange, seeing how she knew someone else's house so well.

I was trying not to pry, not because there was anything wrong with that, but because everywhere felt odd and almost sacred because Greta was gone, and this was where she had lived.

It's so hard not to make a judgment in other people's homes.

Take Bedwyr's room. It was bigger than our entire downstairs at home, and it was perfect. A huge television, the newest computer system, clothes and trainers that I'd die for. His bed was bigger than Mam's, and there was a huge Welsh rugby logo painted above his bed. But there were three days' worth of mugs and plates strewn about, and his nice, new clothes were left on the floor when he was done with them for the day. I couldn't imagine being like that, but I wasn't surprised—people like him never realized how lucky they were.

Lucky? I reminded myself. *Greta's dead!*

"I'm going to the kitchen now, okay? Do a proper job, Shaney, and don't forget the corners." The hoover was one of those expensive ones where you could see the dirt in the machine (which was disgusting but was seen as a good thing for some reason).

"Okay."

"Come and find me if there's anything you're not sure about, all right?"

"I can hoover a bedroom, Mam."

Actually, I was quite good at it. I wasn't that good at cleaning my own room at home—Mam moaned about it a bit—but I had to admit, there was something satisfying about tidying a room until it looked perfect. I was only meant to do the hoovering, but I'd do other little bits, too, like straightening up a pile of books on the shelf, making sure that the bottles and tubes on the table faced the right way, lining up all the pairs of trainers. I finished Bedwyr's room, the spare room, and the living room in no time at all. But I knew that I had to do Greta's bedroom, and the thought of it made my stomach churn—a bit nervous, a bit excited.

I opened her door and sneaked in with the hoover as if I wasn't meant to be here.

Everything was exactly as it had been the last time I was here. Well, almost everything. Shit. Poor Greta.

I could see her now, sitting on that bed, her knees pulled up to her chin, her hair a folded sheet of golden silk but the makeup scarring her eyes and cheeks with black tear tracks.

"What do I do, Shane? Help me!"

I sat on the bed. Someone had been sleeping here—Liz, maybe. The sheets were crumpled, and a soft, slight indentation was on the pillow where someone's head had been resting.

"I'm in too deep. I really can't do this anymore. And I can't tell anyone but you. Please!"

The only time we'd been alone in that house, just her and me. Liz and Kelvin had been away celebrating their wedding anniversary in some city hotel. A city had enough to distract a person from a spouse they'd been ambivalent about for a number of years.

I didn't like Bryn Mawr. Greta looked so much smaller than herself in such a big house. She wasn't herself in her own home.

That was only—what? A month ago? No, a little longer—six weeks. But no one knew I'd been to Bryn Mawr that day. Not Keira or Liz or Mam. No one knew how well I knew this room. No one knew I'd sat on that desk chair, smelling all of Greta's perfumes and trying to make her laugh.

"What are you doing?" she'd asked through her tears as I lined up the bottles, all of them pretty and twinkling like jewels.

"Why aren't the names on the bottles?"

"The names are on the boxes. The bottles are prettier without the names." She wiped away her tears, momentarily distracted from her misery by my unexpected interest in her perfume collection.

I removed the lid from one bottle and sprayed the air before sniffing the tiny droplets that misted down.

"Wow! It's sweet!" I returned the cap. "Like a really horrible bag of sweets that nans tend to like. Basically solid sugar and no flavoring. I call this one Type One Diabetes."

Greta giggled and wiped her eyes with her sleeve.

I reached for the next one.

"Bloody hell, that's spicy and sweet and a bit much. Like someone spilled tikka in a pudding. I know!" I held up the bottle ceremoniously. "I call this one Madras Milkshake."

Greta laughed properly then, a belly laugh, and I couldn't help but grin at her. We rarely had moments like this, except maybe that day in Rhyl—moments when everything felt like it was okay.

I reached for another bottle. "God, this is like that floral-scented stuff they put down the toilet to clean it. This shall forevermore be called Bog Bleach Bouquet."

"You're such an idiot!" Greta laughed and threw a teddy bear at me from the bed. I broke into laughter too. I'd made her happy. Me. I'd made her better.

It was so silent now. All her stuff still here, and Greta gone. It felt like a dead room.

And though my most recent memories of this place were sad ones, I could imagine the normal times here, too, the reality of Greta's everyday life. Things like reaching for the snooze button on her phone alarm clock on a school day, or sitting in front of that mirror, straightening her hair, or lying in that bed, poring over her homework as she listened to music.

Those were probably the things that were on Liz's mind as she lay here at night. She would be thinking about Greta as a little girl, and remembering her on Christmas mornings, and . . .

I picked up the pillow and held it to my face, trying to find a hint of Greta's scent. But she was gone, and in her place was a man's smell. Oily hair and a faint trace of aftershave. I turned my face away—it wasn't a pleasant smell—and put the pillow back exactly where it had been. There was one short, thick strand of blond hair on the pink cover, which told me one thing. It wasn't Liz who had been sleeping here. It was Kelvin.

Mam said I'd done well. She meant it, too, and not in the way that parents admire their kids' artwork when they've done a terrible painting at school. I did the hoovering and dusting, and I emptied the dishwasher. And it was me who offered to empty the small dustbins in the bedrooms. Mam agreed that it was a good idea, and of course it gave me the perfect opportunity to go out into the yard and do the task I had come here to complete.

By the time we left Bryn Mawr that afternoon, Greta's phone and bag had been jammed under the driver's seat of Kelvin's muddy Land Rover—the one that only he drove. The car smelled of diesel and aftershave and something else, something earthy and fresh. There was a discarded chocolate wrapper on the passenger seat and a half-empty bottle of water on the back seat. Otherwise, the interior was spotless.

I used cleaning products from the house to clean my fingerprints off everything.

"Fair play to you. You're very good when you make an effort," said Mam as she drove us home, and it took me a split second to realize that she was talking about my skills as a cleaner, not about my talents in getting rid of key evidence in a murder case.

◆ ◆ ◆

We didn't go for a walk or go out for a coffee. But that night, Mam and I drove to Maccies, ordered Big Mac meals, and went to eat them in that pretty lay-by in Anglesey where you could look out over the straits and the suspension bridge. I'd tried to pay for the meal, but Mam said I deserved it for the work I'd done at Bryn Mawr that day.

"God, this is lovely," she said, chewing on her Big Mac, a bit of that pinkish sauce on her left cheek. "Thanks for helping me today, Shaney."

"It's okay."

"Must have been weird for you, going into Greta's room. Maybe I should have done the cleaning in there. I didn't really think."

"It's fine."

We were silent as we ate, but I sensed that she wanted more from me.

"It's so strange, isn't it? The way people seem to change when they die."

Mam looked over at me. The sky was slowly blackening over the bridge, and the mountains of Bethesda loomed darkly behind Bangor. I couldn't see the quarry from here. You'd never have thought that one of those mountains had been blasted and disemboweled.

"What d'you mean?"

"You know. Because she died young, everyone thinks she was perfect."

Mam stared at me for a long time as I crammed my fries into my mouth. "Was she not like they're saying, then? Greta?"

"No one is like they're saying," I replied, slightly apprehensive that I'd said too much. "Yeah, she probably was. Pretty perfect. I didn't know her *that* well, did I."

CHAPTER 17

The man in the four-by-four was called James Oliver Lewis, and he was thirty-six years old at the time of Greta's death. He lived half an hour away, and that half an hour was a world away when it included a dual carriageway and a mountainous barrier of crags and peaks. He was one of Kelvin's golfing pals and had met Greta when they'd all come to Bryn Mawr for drinks after a game. He was handsome and charming, and although I could only guess what passed between them, I imagine he complimented her, smiled at her, made himself seem good and kind and safe.

It was all Keira's doing. Something about the secret boyfriend of Greta's had stuck with her, like a thorn under her skin—slightly painful, annoying, gnawing at her. Why wouldn't Greta have told her about him? Why did he have to be kept a secret—a secret from *her*, of everybody, Greta's best friend, her constant alibi and someone who never judged?

What the hell made *him* so special?

It takes a whole community of friends to solve the mysteries of a young girl's life, and there were things that Keira noticed that Dion and I, forever on the lookout for anything, didn't see.

She noticed him at the funeral, standing in a line of Kelvin's golf friends. All dressed in black suits, white shirts, and black ties, all of them with that slight sheen of money. He was the youngest of the crew and was handsome in a 1940s Hollywood way—hair parted at the side and slicked neatly, dark eyes, a long, luscious mouth.

That's not why he caught Keira's eye, though. Beauty wasn't impressive to her.

He was crying.

And trying to hide it, even from his friends. Swallowing and swallowing, as if that would make the tears stop coming—but they didn't, and every so often, he was dabbing his eyes with a handkerchief quickly. Keira thought that was weird, but, hey, they *were* at a funeral; people *were* crying. It didn't mean anything. But still, she thought it was strange when, back at Bryn Mawr, where people had gone after the funeral, Keira saw the man stealing glances at the photograph of Greta on the mantelpiece. Swallowing, swallowing, swallowing.

Maybe he's just the sensitive type, thought Keira. *Maybe he has his own daughter at home, and this is just too much for him.* One of Keira's greatest strengths and weaknesses was the fact that she tended to be empathetic. Everyone didn't react the same; everyone didn't feel the same; everyone didn't grieve the same. She was not one to judge, because sometimes, she wondered if people secretly judged her for being hard.

She was never happy with not telling the cops about Greta's lover in the four-by-four. But my argument—that they'd just make her out to be a minxy seductress—always held her back from spilling any information. It was always there, though, that secret, because it felt huge and dark and unknown, and Keira herself only knew part of it. He *could* have murdered her, so easily. It *could* have been him. But Keira had another suspect in her mind, and she focused on him. It couldn't have been *both* of them, after all.

If she hadn't been worried about it, if that black Mercedes four-by-four hadn't been an unanswered question in her mind, she would never have noticed the car. It might have been a coincidence, but

I don't really believe they exist—if something is in your thoughts often enough, you will, eventually, see it.

And it was in such a nondescript place, parked empty in a street in Bangor, outside a pizza place. Keira couldn't have known it was the same one, so she took a few steps forward to see its front windscreen. There was a long, rectangular piece of paper there with some writing on it, like a parking permit.

Bingo.

She waited for its owner to come back, pretending that she was looking at the city flats advertised in an estate agent's window.

And the man from the funeral came out of the pizza place with a girl, and Keira's stomach quivered. She gasped and then turned away, back to the window of the shop, not wanting to be seen.

She looked into the reflection of her own eyes. They looked completely black, and the hazy, unclear image of herself looked older than her years. Behind her, the man and girl got into the car, and the girl was giggling. "Who likes anchovies? You weirdo . . ."

Not his daughter, then, thought Keira. *Daughters know which pizza toppings their dad likes*. And her mind was bubbling with thoughts—why was the man from the funeral driving the Mercedes four-by-four? Did it mean anything? What if it wasn't the same one? Who was the girl?

She very casually turned around, pretending to look at her phone. The Mercedes engine purred into life, but before it moved away, Keira saw the man lean over to kiss the young girl in the passenger seat. She was no more than eighteen, probably younger. Blonde hair. Pretty.

Definitely not his daughter.

She lifted her phone as the car sped away toward the edge of town, and she took a photo. Not that it was proof of anything, but she didn't feel she needed proof.

This was the man.

◆ ◆ ◆

Keira decided to take her aunt's car.

No one would notice—her aunt was at work. She didn't have a license, of course, but she'd had a go a few times in the industrial estate late at night—she knew how to drive. And what were the chances of her getting caught? The police didn't really stop people as long as they didn't do anything terrible. The police had proven to her yet again how inept they were—how come they knew nothing about the man in the Mercedes four-by-four and nothing about the man who drove it? No. If justice was to be done, Keira knew that it was up to her to do it.

Dion sat in the front with her, terminally unafraid and with the slight, frequent tics of an aggressive person who was spoiling for a fight. I sat in the back, seat belt on, an edge of fear in me that Keira was going to kill us all.

She'd told Dion and me about what she'd seen in front of the pizza place. I'd told her that it was no proof of anything—maybe it was a coincidence. What good would it do to say anything anyway?

But Keira was adamant in a way that I secretly trusted. "He was weird at the funeral. He drives the same car as whoever Greta was messing about with. I saw him with another young girl. That's circumstantial evidence, and it's enough for me."

Dion had nodded emphatically. I don't know how much he actually believed or if he just wanted someone to be angry at, but his fists were tight as he listened to Keira. Within a week of her telling us about seeing a car in front of the pizza place, he had the name of the man.

All Dion had done was hang around the golf club for a few hours on a sunny Sunday. He'd taken his phone and huddled down by the trees next to the clubhouse, watching videos on his screen until, right enough, a black Mercedes four-by-four turned up. A man in crisp, clean golf gear got out and opened the boot of his car as other cars turned up. More of Kelvin's golfing gang. Dion huddled down and watched them. There was some gentle teasing about the price of the man's new golf clubs and how his handicap was childlike. Dion knew men like them. They'd be friends but also competitors; they wouldn't know loyalty;

they'd never experienced it. Dion watched and noted their handshakes, their barking laughter, the way it all seemed too easy for them.

Kelvin didn't come. He was still in mourning.

Dion had several plans, the best and possibly most effective being that he was going to wear a wide, fake smile when the men finally left the club after their game. He'd approach the man and say, *Hey, Steve! How are ya?* And then hopefully, the man would say, *Sorry, mate, I'm not Steve; my name is Richard* or *Gruff* or *Howard.* Either that or, upon hearing it, his friends would tease him in that childish, silly way that men sometimes do—*Ha ha ha, it's Stephen, is it, Robbie?* or *This kid thinks Neal's called Stephen!*

The plan wasn't perfect, but he would have found a way. He was like that. Patient. Cold.

But he didn't need to be. Fate was on his side that day, because after they'd disappeared into the clubhouse, Dion took a quick look into the Mercedes four-by-four and saw a parking permit in the window. It was from the hospital where he worked as a consultant. *James Oliver Lewis.*

He also had a child's pink butterfly-patterned car seat and a unicorn blanket in the back of his car. Dion wondered if Greta had ever seen those when she rode with the man. Whether she knew the names of his wife and kids.

"I don't know why we're going," I said as Keira drove us along the dual carriageway. She was a good, sensible driver, checking her mirrors, never forgetting to indicate, never driving too fast. She'd pass her test in no time.

"I've told you, I just want to see."

"We've seen it all on Facebook."

And we had. Once we had a name, we had it all—photos of James and his lovely, grinning, happy wife, Michaela, their beautiful, blonde daughter, Evelyn, and their home in Colwyn Bay, only half an hour away, but a world away too. We'd found Michaela's social media accounts and a post that confirmed what we already knew. An image of a jewelry box containing a pair of tiny stud earrings with pink gems in the shape of love hearts. Exactly like the ones Greta had worn for her school portrait.

He must have given his wife and his lover the same ones at the same time. The picture was posted online about a fortnight before we had our school photos taken.

> Hubster got me a gift for no reason! Got me a good
> one here! #hearts #love #truelove

It was a Saturday afternoon when we took that trip to Colwyn Bay. Keira parked the car at the bottom of their drive. It was a newish house on an exclusive estate, with all lawns perfectly tended, all the houses uniform and tidy. The Mercedes four-by-four was parked outside, as was a little purple scooter with shiny streamers coming out of the handlebars.

Keira wanted to go alone.

We sat in the car watching her. She moved like someone older than herself, I thought, with a purpose and a confidence that you didn't see in girls our age. It was a hot day, and she had a sheen of sweat over her face, but it gave her a made-up look.

Dion sat on his hands in the front seat. "I wish she'd let me look after her," he said.

"She doesn't need looking after."

Keira walked up to the front door and knocked. We watched as a little girl, wearing a rain jacket and a tutu, answered the door. Keira couldn't help it. She smiled at the little girl, complimented her clothes. We couldn't hear a word, although our windows were open, but we could see the expressions, read the exchange. Later, Keira told us what was said.

"Is your dad at home?"

And then he appeared, clutching a mug of something in one hand and holding a tea towel in the other. He smiled for a second, and then his expression faded, as if his spirit was fading when he recognized Keira. He'd seen her at the funeral, of course. She was pretty—the type of girl a man like him would remember.

"Evelyn, go upstairs to play."

And although she was little, Evelyn knew that the change in tone in her father's voice meant that there was no space for disagreement, so she ran upstairs, her tutu streaming around her.

James stared at Keira. He looked terrified.

"I'm Greta's friend." Her voice was a blade. His mouth fell open to say something, but there was nothing. No reason or excuse.

That wasn't good enough for Keira. She stood there, her hands in the pockets of her little leather jacket, staring dead into his eyes. He wasn't going to get away with saying *nothing*.

For being a man in his thirties who wanted a schoolgirl girlfriend.

For making Greta keep him and everything about him a secret.

For being unfaithful to his wife.

For treating girls so badly before he came back home to his own little girl and read her a story before bed, buying her purple scooters and acting like a man who could really feel love.

For whoever that young girl was who had gotten into his car outside the pizzeria.

For being one of *those* men.

"I didn't kill her, I swear . . . ," he said finally, stuttering and pathetic. And Keira, in one swift, elegant move, pulled her hands from her pocket and punched him in the face. The fist of her small, delicate hand was a perfect grenade. His hands flew up to his bleeding nose as she calmly turned around and walked back to the car.

"Dirty bastard," she said, not loudly but enough for him to hear her.

◆ ◆ ◆

Keira was calm in the car for a few miles; then she started trembling. "Jesus," she said, shaking her head. "I can't believe I did that!"

"You were brilliant!" Dion said, who was never really enthusiastic about anything but seemed energized by the sudden, sharp burst of violence. "So calm!"

"My fist hurts," she said, wiggling her fingers as she drove. "His daughter definitely didn't see, did she?"

"No way," I reassured her. "You were heroic, Keira. Greta would be so proud."

"Really? For punching her boyfriend in the face?"

"You know she would." Keira looked at me in the rearview mirror and nodded. Her eyes were shining with adrenaline, and we both knew that things weren't over. She still had a difficult and significant and disgustingly honest conversation to have with the police about Kelvin. That would probably be far more difficult than one single punch to a weak man's face.

◆ ◆ ◆

When the car drove into Bethesda that evening, it was the most beautiful it had ever been.

The pale-orange sunset lit up the houses and the people of our warm, friendly village, like a film. Mothers pushed their babies in prams, hoodies tied around their waists, their hair and faces shining in the pretty light. Old men smoked outside the pub, laughing at one another's familiar jokes, the smell of their tobacco drifting warmly like kind ghosts along the pavements. Young girls walked arm in arm, pretending not to see the young boys; a middle-aged couple walked to the pub together, their shoulders touching as they strolled, having created love and found peace in their familiarity.

The mountains stretched to heaven, looking their very best before the dark.

And the quarry, of course, somehow a more inviting shade of purple in this lovely light. I knew that the slates would be warm this evening, and I hoped someone was up there, walking, touching them as they passed.

I loved Bethesda.

In a way I would never love anywhere, or anyone, again. I loved the stories behind the front doors and the faces in the queues at the shops and the fact that on every street, there was somebody who knew my name. I'd seen so many people saved here, people who had tripped up on life and had been helped back up by a neighbor or a friend of a friend. We knew one another as well as we knew the paths around the quarries and mountains, and we forgave one another for all the times we lost our path.

It was my home, and it cared for me.

CHAPTER 18

Keira waited until she had an English lesson before she went to speak to the police. I didn't mind English, but she hated every second of it, especially when we had to read a book or a play or, worse still, poetry. Some people already have enough stories—they don't need other people's fiction filling their heads.

As soon as Miss Einion said that we were going to be discussing the symbolism in *Macbeth*, Keira's hand shot up in the air. Miss Einion sighed and peered over her glasses.

"I need to go, miss."

"You had plenty of time before the lesson . . ."

"Not to the toilet. I want to go and talk to the counselor."

A few faces turned to look at Keira, but this sort of thing wasn't unusual. Many of the class had avoided boring lessons by pretending that they had to go and talk to the counselor. During physics lessons, there were queues outside her door.

Keira wasn't that type, though. Everyone knew that she was too close to Greta to be able to take any of this lightly, and so the turned heads were because people realized that she might actually really feel the need to speak to someone.

"Yes, of course," said Miss Einion quietly. Perhaps she was worried that she had done something wrong. *Macbeth* is a violent play to be studying with a group of people who had just lost their classmate to a nameless murderer. Perhaps she could have chosen something gentler.

"What's that about?" Dion asked me quietly.

"They were best mates. She gets upset. Don't worry."

I caught Keira's eye as she crammed her books into her backpack. She was going to tell the counselor about Kelvin. A mean, bubbling excitement stirred in the pit of my belly.

Something was about to happen.

◆ ◆ ◆

It only took a few hours for things to begin to move.

Firstly, Keira told the counselor, and then the police, that she had felt uncomfortable with Kelvin. She told them what had happened that night at Bryn Mawr and what Greta had said to her. After some further questioning by a pacing, visibly disturbed, and almost excited Karen, Keira confessed that there were a few other things that felt a bit off about Kelvin and Liz. Like the fact that Greta never wanted to go home. That she spent a large amount of her spare time at Keira's house, including Christmas Eve last year. That she would never answer her phone if it was one of her parents calling. That she'd always describe her parents' relationship as *fucked up* and *dysfunctional*.

(This is all quite normal, of course—who wants to be with their parents all the time? Why would she choose to stay in a farmhouse in the middle of nowhere when she could be warm and cozy in her best friend's home in the village? But everything about Greta's life was a clue now. Everything was evidence that things had not been right at Bryn Mawr.)

After Keira spoke to the police, she asked to go home, saying she was too traumatized to return to classes. The police took her home, where she spent the afternoon bingeing on a box set. There was a biology lesson after lunch. Keira hated biology. She'd settled underneath her duvet, the screen of her laptop in front of her, when unexpectedly she burst into messy, snotty tears.

She had a feeling she was right about Kelvin being a bad, bad man, and that thought was terrifying.

After school, after Mam came home and we had tuna pasta bake and I'd pretended to do my homework, I was sitting on my bed, checking the Premier League table on my phone, waiting for something to happen. Mam was ironing in front of the television downstairs. I heard her swear.

"Bloody hell!"

I went downstairs. She was ironing one of Kelvin's shirts, a pile of clean, pressed clothes from Bryn Mawr on the chair by her side. A few of Kelvin's shirts were hanging up around our living room, as pale and still as hanging men. Through the steam that rose from the iron, Kelvin's face filled the TV screen. He looked like death.

I knew, of course, that this would happen, but I hadn't expected it to happen so quickly. The screen showed a young policeman leading Kelvin out the back door of Bryn Mawr, his eyes wide and his jaw slack, somehow, as if he was screaming with his mouth shut. The TV lights cast a harsh glow over him, and the newsreader's most serious voice spoke over the pictures.

"Kelvin Pugh, father of teenager Greta Pugh, has tonight been arrested on suspicion of her murder . . ."

"My God," exclaimed Mam, shaking her head. *"Him?"*

"Are you surprised?"

Mam snapped her head toward me, her eyes searching. "Well, yes! I know him, Shane! There's no way he did that . . ."

"Really? The things people say about him . . ."

"Like what?"

"You said yourself! He's creepy. And so false . . . thinks he's the big man around town, flashing his cash, thinking that because he owns the mountain, he's actually worth more than—"

"That doesn't mean that he's capable of killing his own daughter!" Mam turned back to the TV, to the man she'd spent time with, the man whose hairs she'd cleaned out of the shower drain, the man who'd made her posh coffees with a warm smile. Something in her was determined to remind herself of the warm, loving feeling she'd had toward this man. That she'd very nearly fallen for him.

"No, but it means that he does put on an act. That no one really knows him. You said yourself a few weeks ago that Kelvin and Liz made you feel sick. Maybe you should trust your gut feelings."

"Nobody really knows anyone," Mam muttered, more to herself than to me, and looked down at the striped shirt she was ironing. *His* striped shirt. She shook her head. "Bloody hell."

"I'm just surprised that they didn't arrest Liz too."

"Stop it. I didn't raise you to be this unkind."

"You're naive. You wouldn't give them the benefit of the doubt if they were broke like us."

"Bullshit!" Mam was more hurt than she was angry, I think. Those words were more painful to her than anything else, and they weren't true—Mam wasn't like that. But everything would be so much easier if she just believed that Kelvin had killed Greta.

"It's true. You see that shirt you're ironing? It costs six times as much as what they pay you to do the ironing for their entire family."

I turned to leave, but not before I took one last look at the screen. In the background, I could see the Land Rover, and inside that Land Rover was enough evidence to have Kelvin Pugh locked up for life.

The school was buzzing with the news the next day, and there were more photographers by the gate. Keira didn't come. She'd sent me a message the night before.

Fuck.

I'd replied, of course, saying that none of this was her fault, that it was only right they investigated who Kelvin really was. But Keira was inherently kind, and she felt guilty for just telling the truth. She saw the best in everyone—that would always be her biggest weakness.

Dion and Gwyn and I were sitting together in our registration class, and the girls had all huddled together to discuss the news. Only Mary sat alone, although she didn't look sorrowful about it that day—her back was slightly straighter as she looked down at the screen of her phone. I wondered if seeing someone punished made her feel better about what had happened to her.

Gwyn, on the other hand, had the lazy, darting eyes of a man whose worries had kept him awake all night. I didn't expect to see him so shocked—he was as pale as morning.

"You look awful," said Dion cheerfully.

"Of course I do!" hissed Gwyn, as if this was all a secret and not being broadcast on all the news channels. "He didn't do it . . ."

"How do you know?" asked Dion, a little too aggressively. I gave him a look, but his eyes were on Gwyn. Dion was trying to seem dis-interested, but I knew him better than Gwyn did, and I could spot the nerves bubbling under his deathly stillness. His eyes locked on Gwyn the way a wild animal locks onto his prey. "Was it you?"

"Don't be so bloody stupid! He's a nice guy, isn't he! We know him!" Gwyn replied, panicked. "Dad was at school with him, and he says there's no way he ever . . ."

"They must have some evidence if they arrested him," I said.

"Like what?"

"I don't know, do I!"

But there *was* a cop that drank in the George pub with Ela's dad, and he wasn't very good at keeping his mouth shut. He had been work-ing behind the desk on the night that Kelvin was arrested and brought in. Once that copper had been bought a few pints, he blabbed to the whole pub.

"What do you have on you?" he asked from behind the police station desk. His voice was monotonous because this wasn't a job you could afford to be emotional about. He also knew that Kelvin would find blankness more terrifying than anything.

Kelvin stared at him across the desk. He was paper pale, the skin on his face like the pages of a faded book, although there were tiny broken veins mapping out paths on his nose as on someone who drinks too much good wine.

"Well?" asked the police officer. Kelvin stared at him as if he was speaking another language.

"Sorry . . ."

"What do you have on you? Wallet? Keys? Phone?"

"Oh!" Kelvin emptied his pockets onto the desk.

A black leather wallet that was packed tightly. Inside, the police officers would find thirty-six pounds and forty-five pence in cash, lots of debit cards—including that gold one you could only get if you were rich, a membership card to the rugby club, a receipt for a ruby necklace from a jeweler's in Caernarfon, a picture of Greta and Bedwyr when they were children, both grinning widely as they stood at the summit of a mountain.

A pocketknife, a good one with lots of different tools—a bottle opener, a corkscrew, several sharp blades. A few thin threads of wool were tangled up in the Swiss Army knife—it was obviously used on the farm. And although Greta was murdered using a heavy object, nobody wanted to be arrested while carrying a knife.

A phone. The most recent iPhone, with a heavy metal case to protect it—not the one that the police had previously searched but a second phone, and unlike the one Kelvin had handed over before, there was more on there than chats about the price of lambs and arrangements to play golf. The wallpaper of this one showed the mountain behind Bryn Mawr, but the really interesting thing about that phone was the messages the police later found on it. Kelvin had deleted them, of course, but only the most stupid people think that it's ever truly possible to get rid of anything once you've typed it into anywhere.

"I want a solicitor!" Kelvin said as the police officer took his phone. And that, of course, was the beginning of the end for him. He sounded guilty, as if he had something to hide. And of course he *did* have something to hide—plenty, in fact—but not the things that the police were searching for.

Because Kelvin didn't kill Greta.

Looking back at the deleted information from Kelvin's phone, the police found that he had been sleeping with one of Liz's friends, as well as Ffion, a smiley girl who worked in Crust Café. Ffion had just turned eighteen. Kelvin had been in a relationship with her for at least eighteen months, and the messages between them were enough to make a room full of police officers blush. The investigators also saw the foul, disgusting names Kelvin called his wife when he was chatting with his friends in an online group—these rich, powerful, respected friends he had—and they saw the filthy, derogatory, sexualized way they all discussed girls of Greta's age.

There were messages from Kelvin to his daughter on the phone too. *Where are you?* Several of those, followed by *Come home now!* And one message, on the night Greta died—*Don't come home then, you whore.* Greta rarely replied, but the few words she sent her father sounded like the death gasps of a person suffocating. *I won't be long. Please, Dad.* And the final message, the last thing Greta communicated to her father before she was brutally murdered.

Please be kinder, Dad.

The plain, ugly truth about any person is to be found in their phone. It's the most truthful mirror anyone has.

After I heard the story of Kelvin's arrest, I often wondered about Call Me Karen and how she felt reading those messages that pointed so clearly in Kelvin's direction. Did she feel the same horror as the rest of us did as the truth of the dysfunctional, messed up relationship between father and daughter slowly revealed itself message by message, stark word by sharp sentence? Or did a part of her feel a thrill, knowing that she'd gotten her man? Was a small part of her jubilant that he'd been so horrible, because it meant that she could charge him?

Kelvin was led to his cell and shut into the cold, bare box. There was nothing in there except for him, a bed, and a toilet, and the police officer stared in at him through the tiny window in the door. What a place for a man like him. His en suite at home was bigger than that cell.

He stood in the center of the room, staring at the wall. He looked pathetic. In the outside world, he was well built, but in there, there was just too much of him. In the outside world, his face was taking on the creases and ridges of the mountain he owned, reflecting his land in a handsome, rugged way—in there, he just looked old. He'd had to remove his shoes in case he would try to hang himself with the laces, and so he stood there in paper slippers, old and overweight and without the comforting feeling of his phone and his wallet in his pocket. A dirty old man, a creep. Weirdo. Perv.

Kelvin stood like that for a long time. Still. Silent. Just stood there, with no idea what he was meant to do now.

He was probably thinking about the fact that he'd lost everything. His wife, his son—Bedwyr wouldn't want anything to do with him after he saw those messages. They'd probably have to sell the farm when the divorce came through. He would lose his mountain.

But he wasn't expecting anything to come of this far-fetched suspicion that he was Greta's killer. Because—as he knew—he didn't do it. There could be no evidence of *that* against him, at least.

He had no idea, of course, about the handbag and phone I'd planted in his Land Rover. How long would it take for the police to find them? Hours? A day at most.

Please be kinder, Dad.

Yes, I made sure that Kelvin Pugh was blamed for the death of his daughter. What was he actually guilty of doing? I'm not sure. But I could remember her tears. I could remember having to hide the fact that I was her friend, in case he got angry. And I remembered the way he'd treated my mam, the way the slight, soft touch of his foot on hers was an act of cruel control.

I had no regrets, not then and not now. Kelvin Pugh did not kill his daughter, but he was guilty of so much.

CHAPTER 19

No one ever really knows another person.

Not really. The Shane that my mother knows is very different from the one that Dion or Gwyn knows. And I was different again with Greta. That's what people are like. We change ourselves in order to fit in with whoever we need to be at any particular time. It's dishonest and manipulative and very normal.

"Why don't you want anyone to know we're friends?" I asked Greta a few months before she died. We were up in the quarry, sitting on a large, flat slab of slate that was warm after a day's sunshine. That's the thing about slate. It's not like other stones. It retains the heat of good weather and stores it for a long while.

"It's not that," Greta said. She was lying on her back, her blonde hair hanging down toward the ground. Her sunglasses were reflecting the sun. Jesus Christ, she was beautiful.

"Well, what is it, then?"

She sat up, resting on her elbows. "You know what Dad's like."

"But the gang! Why do we have to lie to them? Keira and Dion and them?"

"Because Dad will find out. I know he will. And he'll go mad. Sorry."

"I don't get it."

"It's complicated."

"It's bloody weird."

"Oh, God, it's so much more than weird. Weird, I can cope with." Greta sighed and lay down again.

I didn't understand it, not back then.

I didn't understand anything.

This is what you have to understand.

Yes. I killed Greta.

You probably guessed that. But it wasn't because I was a jealous boyfriend. We weren't lovers. I would have liked to be her boyfriend, I think, had she given any indication that she wanted me in that way, but it never felt important, really. It's easy to get a girlfriend. Real friends are far more difficult to come by—friends that you really know, ones that know everything about you. And that's what Greta and I were, in the end—friends. Such close friends that it was safer that no one knew about us.

It was Liz's fault, in a way. None of this would have happened if it wasn't for her.

The last parents' evening. Can you remember? Liz being sickly sweet with my mother and then that low, barbed, pitying comment to her friend. "Poor thing. She's my cleaner." Greta looking up at her mother, knowing full well how snobbish and mean her mother sounded.

And then Greta's eyes turned to mine, and we stared at one another across the school hall. Me, the forgettable, invisible, overgrown boy. She, the beautiful, perfect young woman. For once, I didn't care that she was better than me. Her mother had just pitied mine simply because she was a cleaner. At that moment, I didn't *want* Greta's attention. I didn't *want* her or her snobbish, superior family.

That's probably why she liked me. Because I absolutely despised her mother.

Later that evening, Mam chatted with friends in the hall—old classmates of hers—so I wandered out to the corridor to look at old school photos. I was bored. All the photos were there, long strips of over a century of pupils' faces, still and blank behind glass. I gazed at them, and they stared back silently.

"They're all dead now."

She was by my side. Greta Pugh. Usually, any attention from a girl like her would make me nervous, but her mother's bitchiness still stung, and it made me unreasonably annoyed with Greta.

"Yup," I replied. "Half of them look like they were on their way out already, actually."

Greta turned to look at the faces. She and I were exactly the same height.

"Funny how you can tell which ones were the bad kids," she said. "Like that one, look." She pointed to a round-faced boy in the center of a photo. She was right. His smile somehow showed that he'd been cruel, the kind of grin that turns into a laugh after someone trips over and gets hurt.

"I wonder what happened to him."

"We'll never know." Greta's eyes still searched the boy's face.

I couldn't stop myself. "As long as he didn't become a cleaner, eh?"

Greta sighed and looked at her feet. "Sorry. Mam's like that."

"Not usually. She puts on a good show of being nice to everyone."

"God, yes. You'd think she was everyone's friend, wouldn't you?" Greta turned and leaned against the brick wall. She looked up at me. "You wouldn't believe how many people say I'm lucky to be Liz and Kelvin's daughter. 'Oooh! Your mother's so lovely!'"

I glanced at her. I was surprised, had always thought that Greta got on with her mother, that they were similar.

"You *are* lucky," I said. "You're minted. Your house is amazing. Mam told me."

"Yeah, it is," Greta agreed. "But if you had the choice, Shane, which life would you choose? Yours or mine?"

I was about to reply that I'd pick hers, and then I saw that her eyes were glistening, as if she could cry if I gave the wrong answer. I stared at her. She wasn't the kind of girl that cried. In all the years we'd gone to school together, I'd never seen her upset.

"Yours," I replied, unsure.

"Well, then, you clearly know nothing."

"Yeah, okay, Greta," I started, unsure what to say. Her name felt new on my mouth. We stared at each other.

"Don't tell anyone, okay, Shane?"

I nodded.

"They're bad people. My parents. The fact that I can only ever be their daughter makes me want to give up now."

◆ ◆ ◆

She hadn't spoken to anyone else about it. Just me, and that was only by chance, because of that parents' evening, because I'd heard the voice of the real Greta, her mask having slipped for a short second. She'd only told me because I was the one that had caught a glimpse of who her mother really was, I was the one—the only one—who had anything negative to say about her. It wasn't much to have in common, but it was important to Greta.

Once you started telling the truth, it's not easy to stop.

We'd meet by the river or in the park or up in the quarry. We wouldn't text, because she was scared that her father would find out. Even when it was cold and raining and I was sure that she'd want to stay at home, she'd call our landline from their landline, and would half whisper, "See you in the quarry in half an hour?"

We'd sit under a tree or under one of the bridges over the river. When it was warm, we'd walk, then sit in the shade of one of the dry-stone walls on her father's land—"He hardly ever comes here, y'know; he's not a good farmer"—and we'd chat or listen to music on our phones. Greta cried a lot. Not all the time, but often.

"You need help," I said one day, pressing an old piece of chewing gum into a gap in the stone wall. She was sobbing and hadn't given any explanation other than "Mam. Fucking Mam."

"Help?" Greta asked.

"Yeah. Antidepressants or something. Mam's been taking them forever."

Greta shook her head. "I don't need pills. I need to get away."

"What d'you mean? Running away?"

"We tried that. There's no point anyway. They'd find me."

I sighed. I'd been meeting Greta secretly for months, and even though we'd chat about school and friends and all that, I didn't know why she was so upset all the time. It felt like she was always on the verge of revealing something huge.

"They're annoying, but all parents are. It's just the deal."

Greta looked at me, wounded. "What the hell do you know about it?"

"Sod all, because you don't tell me about it."

So Greta turned to me in the shade of the stone wall, her long blue-jeaned legs crossed like a child's, her pink jumper like a little girl's top. On the other side of the valley, the quarry was a gouged-out bruise.

She told me things.

Liz Pugh, perfect Liz, beautiful, sexy, popular Liz, who was sick with envy of her own daughter. Who called Greta stupid, ugly, and fat, whose nightly bottles of wine made her hateful, who brewed with anger for no reason at all, who made excuses to yell at Greta or punish her. Perfect Liz, who seemed to be an adoring wife to her admiring husband, but who craved attention from any man, every man. Every few years, Kelvin would find out about another affair and would react with rage and sorrow and tears. She'd be forgiven, and then it would happen again. It was the cycle of their married life. Out in public, they'd hold hands, smile at one another. Pretend. Jesus, it must have been so difficult, perfecting that act of happiness.

Kelvin, as we know, wasn't in any place to be preaching about the virtue of faithfulness—he'd had plenty of affairs himself. But the way he kept an eagle eye on his daughter's movements was almost worse than his adultery. He had to know where she was at all times—no boy could come near her. And yet sometimes, Greta would be allowed out with the rest of us, drinking, messing around. It was after those times that her father would come to her room and sit on her bed, kindly demanding to know what had happened to his young daughter. "Did you meet any boys? What did you do?" His face shone strangely as he asked, as though he was excited to hear the story.

"Has he . . . you know . . . ?" I asked Greta. She shook her head.

"He's never done anything like that to me. And Mam hasn't hit me or slapped me or hurt me that way. They haven't done anything I can get help for, Shane."

"That's not true. They're horrible! Surely you can see that."

"Yeah." Greta leaned her body toward mine, and I put an arm around her. Her body was shivering ever so slightly. You won't believe this, but as pretty as she was, I didn't fancy Greta. Not by that point, anyway. Somehow, I liked her too much for that.

"Are they like that with Bedwyr?" I asked, slightly squeezing her thin, frail body with my arm.

"Not really. Mam dotes on him. Dad just sees all the things he doesn't do right. Makes jokes that he's thick and bad at rugby, but you know that kind of joke—it's not funny, and he means it."

We sat there for a long time that day.

I haven't allowed myself to think about this so much. The way she felt in my arms. The small sniffing sounds she made as she cried. The way I could feel her bones through her clothes, thin, frail bones like a bird. I don't let myself remember, because if I did . . .

She was so, so unhappy. And because we were friends, and because I was the only one that knew, and because I cared, I tried to think of solutions.

"Tell a teacher."

"I can't. They won't do anything. Everyone thinks that Mam and Dad are perfect. They'll make out I'm a drama queen, and it'll make things worse."

"Run away."

"What's the point? They'll look for me, and I'd always be looking over my shoulder. What kind of life would that be?"

"Okay, well just stay, then! You've only got another couple of years; you can go to uni! You'll be free."

"No one's ever free of their parents."

One afternoon, under the bridge at Ogwen Bank, Greta and I talked about what might happen if we murdered her parents. I was the one who raised the possibility.

"We could always kill them," I said, keeping my tone light enough to potentially pretend it was a joke. But she knew me too well. She looked up at me as I took a long drag of my cigarette, the water flowing under the bridge, whispering like a thousand secrets as it passed us. She didn't flinch or exclaim or swear as I thought she would.

Her lack of horror was horrific.

She nodded, tired of everything, and said, "We could do that. How would we do it?"

"I dunno. I haven't thought it through."

"A fire, maybe. They've nearly put the house on fire so many times when they're drunk."

"Could be tricky. They could easily get out, and then you'd be exactly where you are now, just with a burned house."

"We could poison them, maybe? I heard about a type of mushroom you can get in the woods . . ."

In the end, it was just too complicated. Greta didn't think she could do it herself, and she didn't want me to do it because she didn't want me to have to live with the guilt of having murdered two people. But not once did she say that she felt it was too much, or wrong, or that she didn't want her parents dead.

◆ ◆ ◆

It wasn't always misery with Greta.

The most painful memories are the ones I don't allow into my mind. I can't think about who she really was underneath all that heartache, because it's just too painful.

Like the way she'd jam half a packet of Tangfastics into her mouth at once because she liked the way the sour sweets numbed her tongue.

Or the way she'd rant about how terrible the novels and poems were that we were reading at school, and then she'd laugh at herself for getting so annoyed about something so pointless, and she'd stand on some rock or a fallen tree or a slab of slate, and she'd dramatically recite the parts of the bad poems that she remembered, making up the rest.

The time we fell asleep among the slates because they were warm and the sun was so bright, and then the way we woke hours later when the sun was beginning to set, the whole palette of the quarry darker than it had been before and the lake beneath us a thick, inky black.

Her beauty. Once, in a lazy, sun-kissed, and slow-moving conversation, I told her that society cared far too much for beauty, and she replied, like a flash, "Yeah, well, so do you." And I'd denied it, of course, but she was right. I so often thought of people as beautiful or attractive or sexy. Every girl I knew would unconsciously be judged according to looks. Even in telling Greta's story, or my own, I described looks far more than was relevant. And I *did* enjoy her beauty, I really did. It soothed me to look at her. Everything about her made me feel a bit better.

The smell of her hair.

Her stubby, bony fingers.

The way she'd say, "Umm . . ." before answering any questions, and the way she'd sing to herself even though she was tone deaf.

"I've heard dogs that sing better than you, Greta."

"Thanks. Love you, Shaney."

CHAPTER 20

Almost six months to the day after Greta was murdered, Kelvin Mark Pugh was charged with her murder. Not only did his messages to his late daughter exhibit possessive and controlling behavior, but her phone and bag were found under the seat of his Land Rover. After making further inquiries, it became clear that Mr. Pugh was a cruel man who enjoyed making young women and girls squirm.

When the case came to court, three women testified that he had made them feel uncomfortable in his company, and there were almost twenty others who claimed to have had similar experiences with him.

Mr. Pugh claimed to have no idea where the bag and phone had come from but suggested that it may have been his wife, Liz, who had murdered their daughter and then attempted to frame him for it. Liz was duly arrested and questioned before being released without charge. But the damage was done. It became clear during the court case that Liz was an insecure, unfaithful woman who had spent years of her life belittling and insulting her young daughter. Liz's life as she had known it was over. In the eyes of the village, she was as guilty as her husband.

Mr. Pugh was sentenced to life in prison. He had no hope of ever being released. He maintained that he had not murdered his daughter, but there was enough evidence of the bad things he *had* done to convince everyone that he was a man capable of doing such a thing. He was a monster. People wanted to believe that he had done it.

Bryn Mawr was put on the market, and it was sold cheaply to a couple who were from somewhere in the south of England. They changed the name of the old farmhouse to the Crag, and for once, no one complained about an old Welsh house being given an English name. Bryn Mawr was a prettier name, but now it sounded like a curse word to everyone in Bethesda.

Liz disappeared. To South Wales, someone said, which made sense because it felt far enough from here to be a different world. Someone said that she'd changed her name, and somebody else claimed that she'd had a nose job and wore a wig so that she wasn't recognized. That seemed a bit far-fetched to me, but true or not, it didn't matter. She was gone. Bedwyr never came back to Bethesda either, and I hoped that wherever he was, he kept a good distance away from his mother.

Gwyn and Ela stayed together. When he had too much to drink, Gwyn would talk about Greta, saying how lovely she had been and wondering aloud whether, if she had lived, maybe something more could have happened between them. After all, he was the last person she had kissed. Of course he never breathed a word of this to Ela, and none of us were cruel enough to tell him the honest truth—whatever would have happened, there would have been no future for Gwyn and Greta.

Mary left the village as soon as the school year ended. On the very same day, I think. She was trying to escape her own history, and no one could blame her for that—Thom the art teacher was still skulking around town, still charming students before picking one to bully. On that last day, when a teacher asked what each of us was planning, Mary was uncharacteristically verbose. "I'm going to Camden Town, and I'm going to work in a clothes stall . . ."

No one else had known about Greta's plans to run away to London, but clearly, Mary did. I wondered how many secret best friends Greta had, how many of us had secretly loved her and then secretly grieved for her.

Keira became very withdrawn during Kelvin's court case. She felt guilty, as if she'd made a fuss about nothing. But once the jury's verdict came back finding him guilty, she seemed to relax a bit, returned to being who she was, and returned to the rest of us too. "You helped put a bad man in jail," Ela said, thinking that she might like to work in law. "Greta would be proud of you."

Dion was quietly proud too. He didn't know the truth, because it was nothing to do with him. But the version he thought to be true was better than the truth, so I allowed him to believe it.

After it happened, you see, Dion thought he knew it all. He thought that he and I shared a huge and terrible secret.

I'm not that kind of man, just so you know. I'm not a murderer. It's just that I murdered someone. It's not the same thing at all.

I tripped and stumbled my way back from the quarry through the thick blackness of night, my body quaking with the shock of what I had just done. My phone rang, vibrating like a thrill in my breast pocket. Dion. I don't know why, but I answered it.

"Where are you?" he asked, and I tried to answer, but my whole mouth and tongue and teeth felt thick and slow, as though my own words might suffocate me.

"Shane? Have you gone home? There's no one left in the park."

"Fuck." The word tripped out of my throat, and Dion knew me well enough to recognize the weight of that one choked syllable. Something was very wrong.

"What's wrong? Where are you?"

"Shit." The moon lit the path through the park, but its open mouth looked shocked, judging me. It had seen everything.

"Tell me where you are, Shane."

"Park." My teeth were chattering. "Quarry path."

"I'm coming."

I wonder what I looked like to Dion that night, stumbling through the trees, covered in blood. Nothing shocked him—he'd seen so much—but he stilled as he saw me, his eyes wide. His face was the same color as the moon.

"Shit. Shitshitshit." He rushed toward me.

He rushed *toward* me. Anyone else would have run away.

"Are you hurt?"

I shook my head.

"You're shaking. Sit down."

I crumpled down into the moss beside the path, and Dion stood over me, staring. It was cold, and steam was rising like smoke from his mouth.

"Who?" he asked.

"Greta," I replied weakly. His eyes widened.

"Is she . . . ?"

I nodded.

"Shhhhit."

I was soaking with sweat, although I felt the cold too. I'd done it. I'd just done it.

"What happened?"

And I told him exactly what Greta had told me to say.

"Her dad."

"What?"

"We were in the quarry. Greta and me."

"Did you get off with her?"

"Yeah. Gwyn was getting on her nerves."

"And?"

"Her dad turned up. I hid, he never saw me. He was screaming at her. Shit. I feel sick."

"It's fine, you're okay. You'll be okay."

"Calling her a whore and all that. Saying that she slept with everyone. He was mental, Dion; I've never seen anyone like that."

"And he killed her."

"With a piece of slate. Shit, Dion, she went down so quickly. And he just left her there. Drove off. He didn't even cry."

Dion started pacing, a wild animal cooped up.

"I went to her. I had to; I didn't know if she was still alive. Her face was all caved in." I reached out my hand, showed Dion her handbag. "I brought this."

"Fuck! Okay, okay." Dion paced quicker, back and forth, back and forth. "You've got to get rid of that."

"Eh? Why?"

"Because *everyone* is gonna think that you killed her, Shane! Don't you see?"

"I'll just go to the cops! Tell them what I saw!"

"Oh, yeah, okay, because they're gonna believe somebody like you from the estate over a minted farmer like Greta's dad? Come on!"

"What am I supposed to do, then?" I sounded panicked, although I had a vague plan in my mind.

"Throw the bag into the river."

"You reckon?"

"Yes!"

"But . . . wouldn't it make more sense to keep it?"

"No, it bloody wouldn't! You're mental." Dion rushed toward me, but I pulled the bag back into my lap.

"Because if no one believes that Greta's dad killed her, at least we'll have this. If we're desperate."

Dion became still, thought about it. I don't think he was thinking straight at the time either, poor bloke. I had implicated him in all this without even considering it.

"I think we should get rid of the bag. You can't keep it in your house, can you!"

"I won't. I'll hide it. Doesn't matter where, but I'll hide it."

"Fine. But look. We're gonna have to go home before someone realizes something's up. And you're covered in blood, mate."

"Am I?"

I looked down and saw stains on my white hoodie. It didn't look like blood. It looked black.

It smelled like meat.

"It's on your face too."

And that's when I realized that I could taste her blood. It had dried stickily over my face and lips.

I turned and threw up into the moss.

I will never ever find a friend as faithful as Dion. He was the one that pulled my hoodie over my head when I was shaking too much to do anything, and he was the one who used the sleeve to wipe the blood from my face and hair, the thick cotton soaked in the water of the Ogwen river.

We stood by the water, Dion washing my face, like an odd, warped sort of baptism. Neither of us were crying, but tears were streaming from our eyes. He because Greta was dead, and I because I couldn't imagine why Dion loved me enough to be this good a friend to me.

He wore the bloody hoodie under his own so that no one would see the blood. He was the one who went home after sending me on my way, and he was the one who peeled off the hoodie—the only piece of concrete evidence against me—and made sure it went into next door's bin a few days later, on the very day that the bin men came to take away the rubbish. If anyone had caught Dion with that, if anyone had seen us together . . . but he never once hesitated in helping me.

Because Mam was a cleaner at Bryn Mawr, I guessed that the police were sure to come and question her at some point. The bag and phone weren't safe in our house. But I didn't want to get rid of them, because I knew that they'd be useful. And so I hid them in the Welsh class storeroom because that was the last place anyone would expect to find them. Behind some books, unread for decades. They could have stayed there for years, and no one would have found them.

Yes, Dion knew that I had planted the evidence in Kelvin's Land Rover. But he never once asked me whether I had killed Greta. Either the thought never crossed his mind or he felt that if I had done it, he forgave me, both for the murder and the lie I had told him. That's what good friends do. They think the best of you.

◆ ◆ ◆

After Kelvin Pugh was sent to prison, Dion seemed to be happier, better. "I know that we lied, but the right man's locked up now, isn't he. That's the important thing."

I agreed, and I meant it too. I think it was the first time in his life that Dion felt he could make a difference to anything. He mattered. So he tried to make something of himself, and after the exams, he went to college to train to be a mechanic. He was a good, good man. He'd still come over a lot, and we still went to the park at the weekends until we got old enough to drink legally, and then we switched to the pub. But a part of us both will always be those two young men on the riverbank under a dumbfounded moon, washing blood from white cotton and agreeing, without having to say it, to keep a lifelong secret.

Once, years and years after we left school, we were sitting in a beer garden in Bangor, nursing a couple of pints, when we saw Mr. Lloyd and his wife. We went over and said hello. He looked older than his years, but he still smiled like he meant it.

"You were good to me," said Dion. "I didn't get good grades at school, but you taught me a hell of a lot."

"It was never really about the grades," replied Mr. Lloyd, and I thought that he was right and was relieved that he was still someone I'd like to be like.

Everything was the same for Mam and me. Getting away with murder doesn't change your life as much as you'd expect it to. I struggled a bit during the court case because little details were released that reminded me of everything, reminded me of what I'd done. I started having nightmares, and I messed up my exams. But I never felt regret about what I'd done, not once. Liz and Kelvin Pugh were bad people. I was glad that life paid them back for the way they'd treated their daughter.

But God, I missed her.

Not the girl that was on the front pages. Not the perfect, pretty angel that everyone prayed for in school assemblies, not the girl that had a bench dedicated to her memory on the green in front of the school.

No.

I missed the girl who fell asleep on warm slate, the purple quarry a throbbing bruise around her. I missed the girl who smoked with me under bridges and listened to bad '80s pop songs on her phone.

You want to know what happened. I know you do. This is what you've been hoping for—this is why you're still reading. Which is strange, isn't it? If you ask me, people's preoccupation with death is a perversion, especially when it's a violent death, especially when the victim is young and blonde and pretty.

You're going to judge me. But just so you know, I'm judging you too. Because *you* are still reading.

CHAPTER 21

"Come after me, okay? On the quarry path."

That night, in the park. Greta spoke the words under her breath, and I was pissed and pissed off. Bored with having to hide the fact that we were friends. Bored with being afraid of her father. I wanted our friends to know.

Bored with my own obedience. Because I knew that no matter how annoyed I was, I would follow her.

Greta disappeared into the darkness, drunk and loose limbed. I considered not going after her, but Gwyn came from behind the trees, looking at her disappearing into the darkness.

"Was that Greta?"

"She's going to meet someone, I think."

Gwyn nodded, drunk enough to not bother concealing the disappointment on his face.

I followed her. Of course I did. She was my friend. I caught up with her in the heather.

"Gwyn was looking for you."

She turned to look at me. Her eyes seemed black and her skin pale, almost translucent.

"I got off with him. Dad will go mental if he finds out."

"With Gwyn?!"

She nodded, drunk.

"Didn't think he'd be your type." It stung. I wasn't expecting anything from her, but I wasn't expecting her to do *that* either.

It would have been better with me.

"He's so *simple*, Shaney. And *young*. Not his age, you know what I mean. He's a kid. I wanted to know what it would be like."

We walked in silence for a bit. She was crying again, sniffing all the time, but we were drunk, and she always cried, so it didn't seem like a big deal.

"Are you angry?" she asked after a while.

"About you and Gwyn? Nah." And it was true. If I ever had done, I didn't feel like that about her anymore. "You okay?"

"Are you gay?" she asked, her voice slowed down by all the alcohol.

"Dunno. Why are you crying? Where we going?"

"Quarry."

"It's late, Greta."

"Doesn't matter, does it."

So we walked, the moon watching us as we went. Out onto the lane and up the winding road to the quarry, past the zip line, our feet crunching over the shards of slate. That's where she stopped and looked down to the lake, a tarry black mass of nothingness. The moon didn't reach that far into the mountain.

"Careful!" I warned. "You're drunk; you could slip."

Greta turned to me. Her eyes were shining.

"Sorry, Shaney."

When something terrible is about to happen, the world around you warps and changes. Everything becomes sharp, the details clear and still. I was suddenly sober.

"What d'you mean?"

"I just can't."

"Can't what?"

"Go on. Dad's getting worse. He made Keira feel horrible . . . I don't know what he did, but I can imagine."

"That man's disgusting. You've got to tell someone!"

"I can't, Shane. I don't have the strength."

Even though she was drunk and it was late, and even though I knew that this was far more than I could cope with, I could also tell that Greta was confessing a deep, sincere truth. I could hear the finality in her voice, and I knew that I didn't have the words to convince her to change her mind.

She was going.

"You're gonna jump?"

"Only if you don't help me."

I stared at her. The blackness within her felt solid and thick. "Help you?"

"I'm going to die tonight, Shane. Either I jump down into the lake, or you kill me."

"Kill you! Don't be stupid!"

"If I jump, no one will know what things were like. What he was like with me, and Keira, and even Mam, and whoever else he hurt. No one will know who my mother really is. They'll say I was depressed and isn't it sad, and they'll use my name to make a point about depression in young people. It'll be a tragedy, no more than that."

"But that's the truth!"

"But if you do it . . . if you do it, and Dad gets the blame . . ."

"What!" I exclaimed. She was nuts. But she seemed so reasonable, and I wondered if it was me who was crazy and that she made perfect sense. "Look, we'll talk about it, okay? We'll make a plan. And then if this is what you want still . . ."

"No! Here. Tonight. You help me or you don't. It's up to you. I understand if you can't."

"Greta!"

"Everything will point to Dad, Shane. He'll get done for it. I don't want him to get away with everything. I want him to suffer. And if he suffers, Mam will suffer too."

"Has anything happened?" My voice was jittery, quaking. I was crying. "Has he done anything?"

"Don't ask me that." She let out a quick, gasping sob before steadying her voice again. "Just help me. Please."

She chose the slate. A long, rectangular slab. I just stood there, frozen by the thing I knew I was about to do. It felt horribly inevitable, as if I could never have refused. All those meetings between us, all those sweets and cigarettes and tears—it felt like it could only ever have led to this. Had she been planning it? Is this why she befriended me in the first place? Because I was vulnerable enough to do this?

Greta carried the slate over to me and placed it by my feet as carefully as she would have laid down a newborn baby.

"Sorry, Shaney."

She opened her arms and held me, her arms tight around me. She was comforting me for what I was about to do to her.

We held one another tight, and I knew, even if I lived to be old, even if I loved many people and had a full, happy, fulfilling life, that I would never know anyone as well as I knew this girl.

"Do it now."

I picked up the slate. It felt like flesh, somehow still warm from the kind, hot day.

"Thank you, Shane."

I thought about Kelvin, the way he'd made Greta feel, all the things I imagined he'd done to her, the things she couldn't bear revealing to me.

I thought about the way he'd made lovely, sweet Keira feel horrible . . . and who knew what else he'd done to her.

He was the one who would suffer most now.

I lifted the slate above my head, and as I smashed it down, Greta's arms shot up over her head. She couldn't help it. A human's natural instinct is to protect themselves.

◆ ◆ ◆

Sometimes even now, I wake up in the still of the dark hours, my body drenched in sweat.

Everything's easier in the daytime. In the waking hours, I can convince myself that I did the right thing—that Greta had created a way to justice by convincing me to do what I did. There could never have been another way.

But I know as well as you do that I'm lying to myself. It wasn't right.

At night, my mind is too exhausted to battle the truth. I fall asleep easily but wake up a few hours later, my heartbeat filling the silence, my bedclothes drenched in sweat. In those moments, I am certain, utterly certain, that what I did that night was wrong, evil. I will never forgive myself.

Not for killing her. She would have jumped, I'm sure of that—but I didn't save her. I had the chance, and I didn't take it. At the time, I didn't know how, and now—bloody hell—now, I can see all the things we could have done together, Greta and I, to get her out of it.

If she had told a teacher . . .

If she had just stopped pretending she was okay. If she'd cried at school like she'd cried with me. Allowed herself to look as awful as she felt. Stayed behind after a Welsh lesson and said, in a small voice, *Miss, can I talk to you . . . ?*

Of course, sometimes, I think it should have been me saying those things, taking responsibility for her. But that's not quite right either. One person cannot save another. That's not the way the world works, even though the films and books and songs tell you differently.

The most important word in the world isn't *love* or *happiness* or *contentment* or any of those other dull, meaningless words they paint on little hearts made of wood or slate. It's not a word you'd see on a T-shirt or a mug.

The most important word in the world is *help*.

We all miss her. Some of us silently, alone, and others as if they feel the need to prove that they remember her by talking about her all the time. Ela posts photos of her online, with heart emojis and crying emojis. We still see each other, although not as a group. It feels like someone's missing, as if we're waiting for someone else to arrive. All of us sit facing the door, facing the outside. We can't help it.

The moon watched open mouthed as I beat my dear, lovely, complicated, damaged friend and then stared at her broken face, which looked like someone else. I stilled. The echo of the quarry fed my own sounds back to me, the gouged-out mountain bashed in and broken.

In my hands, the slate was as smooth and warm as flesh.

ACKNOWLEDGMENTS

Thanks to all at Y Lolfa and Amazon Crossing, especially Meinir Wyn Edwards, Alexandra Torrealba, Lauren Grange, Faith Black Ross, Harriet (Hattie) Hammersmith, Alicia Lea, and Erin Fitzsimmons.

To Christopher Combemale at Sterling Lord Literistic, for his encouragement, hard work, and enthusiasm.

The Welsh Books Council and the Wales Literature Exchange, who work tirelessly to champion Welsh writers. I am immeasurably grateful.

I Efan, Ger, a Morfudd am fod mor amyneddgar, annwyl, a hwyliog. TTF am byth. x

I Robin. Diolch. x

ABOUT THE AUTHOR

Photo © 2022 Geraint Lleu Ros

Manon Steffan Ros is one of the preeminent writers working in the Welsh language today. She has won many major literary prizes in Wales, and two of her books and one of her plays are featured on the Welsh national curriculum. Her first international English translation, *The Blue Book of Nebo* (translated by Steffan Ros), was published by Deep Vellum in the United States in 2021 and in thirteen other languages. It won the 2023 Yoto Carnegie Medal for Writing in the United Kingdom.